The Search for
the Silver Persian

"We should find some seats," Nancy said to her friends Bess and George. "The showing of long-haired cats is about to start."

"Purrfect's a shoo-in," Bess declared as the three girls sat down. "All she has to do is bat those big green eyes at the judge."

A few minutes later a heavyset man appeared on the stage. "Ladies and gentlemen," he said, "we're about to start the showing of long-haired breeds. Will you all take your seats so that we can—"

Just then there was a scream from backstage, and Nancy's friend Andrea came running out through the velvet backdrop. She dashed up to the heavyset man, waving her arms frantically.

"Somebody has stolen my cat!" she cried.

Nancy Drew
Mystery Stories

Available from MINSTREL Books

NANCY DREW MYSTERY STORIES®

114

NANCY DREW®

THE SEARCH FOR THE SILVER PERSIAN

CAROLYN KEENE

A MINSTREL® BOOK

PUBLISHED BY POCKET BOOKS

New York   London   Toronto   Sydney   Tokyo   Singapore

This book is a work of fiction. Names, characters, places, and incidents are either products of the author's imagination or are used fictitiously. Any resemblance to actual events or locales or persons, living or dead, is entirely coincidental.

A MINSTREL PAPERBACK *ORIGINAL*

A Minstrel Book published by
POCKET BOOKS, a division of Simon & Schuster Inc.
1230 Avenue of the Americas, New York, NY 10020

Copyright © 1993 by Simon & Schuster Inc.

Produced by Mega-Books of New York, Inc.

ISBN: 0-671-79300-4

First Minstrel Books printing August 1993

10 9 8 7 6 5 4 3 2 1

NANCY DREW, NANCY DREW MYSTERY STORIES, A MINSTREL BOOK and colophon are registered trademarks of Simon & Schuster Inc.

Cover art by Aleta Jenks

Printed in the U.S.A.

Contents

THE SEARCH FOR
THE SILVER PERSIAN

1

Opening Day

"Come here, Rover. Come here, kitty," Nancy Drew called out. She wriggled her fingers invitingly toward the neighbor's kitten, who was stranded on one of the highest branches of the Drews' oak tree. "Come here, Rover. *Please.*"

Just then, the Drews' housekeeper, Hannah Gruen, poked her head out the front door. "Who are you talking to, Nancy?"

"Oh, hi, Hannah," Nancy replied. "Rover is stuck way up there, and I'm trying to rescue her."

Hannah nodded knowingly and went back inside.

After a moment Hannah reappeared, bearing a can of tuna and a can opener. Then she stood under the tree and began to open the can. Rover stood up and stared at her, her green eyes suddenly alert.

1

Seconds later the kitten began scampering down the tree, hopping nimbly from limb to limb.

Hannah put the can down and motioned to Nancy that they should back away. When they'd done so, Rover made the final leap to the ground and began devouring the tuna.

"Hannah, you are a genius," Nancy pronounced.

"It runs in the family," Hannah said. "Speaking of which . . ." A car was turning into the driveway. It came to a halt, and a moment later Carson Drew emerged, briefcase in hand.

"Are the two of you having a conference on the front lawn?" he called out.

"Sort of," Nancy replied with a smile, and proceeded to tell her father about the rescue mission.

Carson looked at Rover, who was still chipping away at the tuna. "Cats keep popping up in my life today," he remarked.

Nancy's blue eyes sparkled. "What do you mean, Dad?"

"Let's all go inside and I'll tell you about it," he replied.

When the three of them had settled in the living room, Carson opened up his briefcase and took out the current issue of *River Heights Today* magazine. On the cover was a picture of a hairless cat.

"Am I seeing things, or is that cat bald?" Hannah asked.

Carson grinned. "It's bald, all right. It's some

sort of exotic breed. You see, the lead article is on the big cat show that's coming to town."

"I read about it in the paper," Nancy declared. "It sounds like a lot of fun."

"I'm glad you think so, because I was going to ask you if you'd like to go," Carson said.

"There isn't some mystery involved, is there?" Hannah murmured, an anxious look crossing her face. Hannah had helped raise Nancy since she was three, when her mother had died. Hannah felt very protective toward the girl, especially when it came to her work. At age eighteen, Nancy was an accomplished detective who'd solved dozens of difficult, often dangerous cases.

Nancy pushed back a strand of reddish-blond hair and smiled eagerly. "How about it, Dad? Am I being recruited for a new assignment?"

Carson Drew was a well-known lawyer and sometimes used his daughter's investigative skills. "Well, I have to admit that it's connected to one of my clients, but not in the way you think," he replied. "You see, this man—Mr. Birch—is a promoter for the cat show, and he's offered me some free passes. I'm tied up, so I thought that you and your friends might like to go."

"Great!" Nancy exclaimed. "I'll call George and Bess right away."

It was opening day of the Great Midwestern Cat Show, and the River Heights Civic Center was bustling with activity.

3

"Have you ever seen so many cats in your life?" Nancy declared.

"This place is amazing," George Fayne, Nancy's friend, agreed. "What do you think of it, Bess? Bess?" The slender brunette turned to see where her cousin Bess had gone, but she was nowhere to be found.

Suddenly blond-haired, blue-eyed Bess Marvin appeared out of the crowd, plate in hand. "I went over to the refreshment stand," she said. "All the food has a cat theme. See, this is a Puss-in-Fruits." She held up a strange-looking dessert for inspection. It was a wobbly lump of pink pudding shaped like a cat, with grapes for eyes and ears.

George grinned. "I should have known where to find you, even though we did just eat lunch."

"It's for a good cause," Bess protested. "All the food money goes to finding homes for abandoned cats. Besides, this place is so enormous the calories will get burned off in no time."

Nancy regarded her two best friends with a knowing smile. She was used to their bantering. "Let's get started," she said cheerfully. "We have a lot to see."

The girls contemplated the many aisles of exhibitors' booths ahead of them. Each booth featured one or more show cats, which were kept in large wooden cages for public viewing.

Programs in hand, the three friends headed for the first aisle. They stopped in front of a cage containing a tailless white cat.

4

"No tail!" George exclaimed. "I wonder what kind of cat it is?"

Nancy pointed to a small sign at the bottom of the cage. "His name is Cotton, and he's a Manx," she noted. "The *River Heights Today* article mentioned Manx cats. It said they're called that because they're from the Isle of Man, off the coast of England."

Bess extended a hand toward him. "Hello, Cotton."

Cotton poked his small pink nose through the bars and sniffed, then meowed in a soft, sweet voice.

"Isn't he a darling?" Bess murmured. "I wish I could give him a treat."

George was admiring several Burmese kittens in the next cage. "Cocoa, Mocha, and Bonbon," she said. "Well, what else are you going to name three chocolate-colored cats, right? And check out this cat in the cage next to them. It doesn't have any hair!"

"There was a cat just like it on the *River Heights Today* cover," Nancy said. She bent down to look at the sign on its cage. "He's called a Spinx, and his name is Alabaster."

"Isn't he strange-looking?" George said. "He doesn't even have any whiskers." Alabaster blinked at her and meowed loudly. "Oh, I'm sorry, Alabaster, I didn't mean to hurt your feelings."

Bess had moved on to the booth across the

aisle. "Look at this one," she said. "What a beauty!"

Nancy and George joined Bess. There was only one cage at the booth, and inside was a large, emerald-eyed cat grooming itself. It stopped to give its three admirers a haughty glance, then returned to its long, luxurious, silver fur. Its rhinestone collar glittered in the dim interior of the cage.

"You're right, Bess—this cat's a knockout," Nancy agreed.

Bess peered at the sign on its cage. "She's a Persian named Purrfect. I wonder if she'll take the top prize."

"Her little house should, anyway," George commented, indicating the crocheted rug, velvet pillows, and gingham ribbons adorning Purrfect's cage. "It's fancier than my bedroom."

"Hello!" A petite young woman was walking toward the girls. She had freckles, sparkling brown eyes, and long red hair that she wore in a ponytail. Her black sweater and jeans were covered with silver cat fur.

"Hi," Bess said. "Is this your cat?"

"She sure is," the woman replied.

"We were just admiring her," George explained.

The woman squinted at George. "Say, you look familiar. In fact, you all look familiar. Do we know each other?"

Nancy's face lit up. "You're Andrea, aren't you?"

6

"That's right," George said, nodding. "You used to baby-sit us."

The woman broke into a smile. "And you're Nancy Drew, Bess Marvin, and George Fayne, all grown up. Isn't that incredible? I haven't seen you girls in ages." She turned to Nancy. "I've been following your exploits in the papers, though. You're a famous detective now."

"Well, I've solved a few cases," Nancy said modestly.

"A few cases, my foot," Bess said. "Why, Nancy is single-handedly responsible for—"

"Now, Bess," Nancy broke in, blushing.

"Do you still live in River Heights?" George asked Andrea.

Andrea nodded. "In fact, I'm one of the few locals at this show. There are people here from all over the country, even all over the world."

"Yikes," George said. "That explains the huge crowd."

"Is there anything special we should see?" Nancy asked.

"Well, right now you're in the main hall of the auditorium, where the exhibitors have their cats set up for public viewing. After you're done going up and down a few aisles, you might consider sitting in on some of the showings. There will be a number of them over the next several days. They're held in those galleries." Andrea pointed to a dozen small rooms around the sides of the auditorium.

"Each showing is devoted to a certain category," Andrea explained. "Long-haired breeds, short-haired breeds, and the individual breeds such as Siamese, Persian, and Maine coon. The cats in each category get ranked by a judge."

"By the galleries, you mean those rooms with the folding chairs?" Bess said hopefully. "I'm dying to give my feet a rest."

"What about all those calories you're trying to burn off?" George chided.

Her pretty cousin frowned. "Oh, right."

Nancy turned to Andrea. "There's a Grand Competition on the last day of the show, right?"

"Yes, that's when they pick the best overall cat. Purrfect and I are keeping our fingers crossed."

"I bet she's already won lots of shows," Bess remarked.

"Actually, this is Purrfect's first major competition," Andrea replied. "I'm really just an amateur cat exhibitor, not like these other pros. But I'll let you all in on a secret: Purrfect is going to be in a TV commercial."

"A TV commercial?" George repeated.

"Did Purrfect win a contest or something?" Bess asked Andrea.

"Not exactly. A friend of mine knew someone at Simon-Ross Media, an advertising agency here in River Heights. She found out that they were looking for a Persian for their new Kitty Classics cat food campaign, and one thing led to another. The spot is due to start airing—"

"I'd like to talk to you about that, Andrea," a loud male voice broke in.

The four women turned and saw a tall man with curly blond hair standing nearby. He studied Nancy and her friends coolly.

"What are you doing here, Tad?" Andrea said nervously. "Oh, I'm sorry. Nancy, Bess, George, this is my . . . husband, Tad Cassidy. Tad, I used to be their baby-sitter when they were kids."

Tad ignored the introductions and looked pointedly at Andrea. "About this commercial . . ."

Andrea shifted uncomfortably. "This isn't the time, Tad. I have to get Purrfect ready for a showing."

Why did Tad seem so upset about the commercial? Nancy wondered. It sounded like a good deal. And why was Andrea putting him off?

In any case, Nancy thought that it might be best for the three of them to leave Andrea and Tad alone. But just as she opened her mouth to say goodbye, a commotion erupted in the next aisle.

They all turned to look. A short, fair-haired man with a pencil-thin mustache was shouting at a nervous-looking young brunette.

"Incompetent customs officials!" the man exclaimed. "We should have been here hours ago!"

"I wonder who he is," George said.

"I think that's Sean Dunleavy," Andrea replied. "I've seen his picture in the cat magazines. He's a well-known breeder from London." She lowered her voice. "I've heard he's very—well, arrogant. He wins all the shows.

9

"That young woman must be his assistant," Andrea continued, indicating the brunette. "Poor kid. It must be hard to work for someone like that."

Nancy noticed that Tad seemed to have little interest in Sean Dunleavy's affairs. In fact, the scowl on Tad's face told her that he was as impatient as ever to speak to Andrea.

Nancy peered at her watch. "Two o'clock! Bess, George, we've got to get moving if we're going to see all these cats."

"It was great seeing you all again," Andrea said. "Come by later when you have time, and you can pet Purrfect. She acts very aloof, but she's a sweetheart when you get to know her."

"Bye, Andrea, Tad," Nancy said, noting that Tad had remained silent. Purrfect isn't the only one who's aloof, she thought.

As the three friends walked away, George whispered, "What was going on there? You could cut the tension with a knife."

"I know it," Bess said. "I guess they were having a little marital spat."

Nancy frowned, saying nothing.

"Where to next?" George said.

Nancy scanned the auditorium. "I need to find a phone booth. I promised Hannah I'd give her a quick call about something."

At that moment an announcement came over the loudspeaker. "Ladies and gentlemen, the Manx showing will be held in gallery one in ten minutes. Please assemble in gallery one for the Manx showing."

"The tailless cats!" Bess exclaimed. "Can we go watch?"

"You guys go ahead," Nancy said. "I'll make my call, then join you there in a second."

"All right, Nan," George said.

While George and Bess made their way to gallery one, Nancy found a phone booth and called home. After she had finished, she wandered back into the crowd and started down a busy aisle.

She looked around, trying to get oriented in the bustling auditorium. Just then she spotted Andrea in the next aisle. Nancy was about to go over and ask her for directions when she saw that the young woman was still talking to Tad. Not wanting to interrupt them, Nancy hesitated.

Observing them from behind a booth, Nancy realized that they were having an argument, even though she couldn't hear their words. Tad was red-faced, and he was gesturing furiously with his hands. Andrea was shaking her head and turning away from him.

Then suddenly Tad shouted, "I will get my cat back from you one way or another!"

2

The Cat Vanishes

Nancy watched as Tad spun on his heels and stormed off. Andrea looked very troubled. She stood there pale and trembling, staring at the floor.

Nancy cut over to Andrea's aisle. "Andrea," she called out.

The young woman raised her head. "Oh, hi, Nancy."

"Are you all right?" Nancy asked her worriedly. "I heard you and Tad arguing."

"I'm fine," Andrea replied shakily. "It's just that . . . well, Tad's just found out about Purrfect's TV commercial, and he's very upset."

"What do you mean, he just found out? Were you going to surprise him or something?"

Andrea sighed. "You see, Tad and I are separated," she explained. "When we were first married, Purrfect was Tad's kitten. But over the years she grew more attached to me, so when Tad and I split up, he was happy to let me have her. But now . . . now that Purrfect is about to embark on a big new career and bring in some money, Tad's decided he wants her back for himself."

"That's terrible!" Nancy exclaimed. "How did he find out about the commercial?"

Andrea shrugged. "A few of the people here know, and Tad may have overheard them talking about it. Or maybe my friend Laura—the one who hooked me up with Simon-Ross Media in the first place—told him. She's friends with Tad, too."

"Listen, Andrea, he's just stirring up trouble. He can't take Purrfect away from you," Nancy reassured her.

"I know," Andrea said, sighing. "I just didn't need that argument now, on the first day of the show." She looked at her watch. "Oh, dear, I have to get Purrfect ready."

"For the showing?" Nancy asked.

Andrea nodded. "There's a special showing for long-haired breeds at four o'clock. Purrfect will be up against a dozen other cats. I hope you girls can stick around. It'll be in gallery three."

"We'll make a point of it," Nancy promised. "Is there anything I can do to help? Everyone here seems to have an assistant or two, but you're all on your own."

13

Andrea's face lit up. "That would be great, Nancy. Thanks. Here, you can hold her down while I brush her." She opened Purrfect's cage and picked up the half-sleeping cat. Purrfect opened one emerald eye and meowed disgruntledly.

"Okay, Nancy, put your hand on her back— like this—while I groom her tail." Andrea demonstrated, and Nancy complied. "Purrfect can get very fidgety, so it's good to have you here to keep her still."

While Nancy held Purrfect down on the table, Andrea sprinkled white powder on the cat's luxurious tail and ran a comb through it.

"It's okay," Nancy told the cat soothingly. "We're making you beautiful."

"Now, let's take the collar off so we can do her ruff," Andrea said.

"Her ruff?" Nancy repeated.

"The fur around her neck," Andrea explained. "We have to get it fuller and fluffier, so it forms a kind of halo around her face."

Andrea removed Purrfect's collar, a leather band studded with glittery rhinestones, and proceeded with the combing.

"So what do you do when you're not managing Purrfect's career?" Nancy asked Andrea.

"Oh, this and that," Andrea replied cheerfully. "Mostly I'm a free-lance writer."

"Do you write books?"

Andrea shook her head. "Magazine articles. Right now I'm doing a piece for *Famous Felines*."

14

"Famous Felines?" Nancy grinned. "It sounds like a celebrity gossip magazine for cats."

"You're pretty close," Andrea said. "They mainly do stories about championship cats, but from time to time they also cover the cats of celebrities—you know, movie stars, politicians."

Purrfect glanced up and meowed loudly. "Okay, okay, we're finished," Andrea told her, putting the comb away.

"She looks like a winner to me," Nancy declared.

"Thanks so much for all your help," Andrea said gratefully. "And thanks, too, for listening about Tad. It's nice to have a friend here."

Nancy patted her arm sympathetically. "No problem. Just remember—Purrfect is your cat. There's nothing Tad or anyone else can do about that."

Gallery one was a room with folding chairs, a stage, and a velvet backdrop. On the stage the Manx showing was well under way. A judge was holding a tailless gray cat in the air, examining its form. Behind the judge was a row of cages, each of which held a Manx. The cats' owners hovered anxiously off to the side.

"You missed the first half," Bess said to Nancy in a low voice. "All the cats looked like Cotton, except that they come in different colors—black, brown, cream."

Nancy explained about the argument between Tad and Andrea.

15

"What a rotten thing to pull," George murmured. "Well, I hope Purrfect wins the Grand Competition and gets in a hundred commercials and makes Andrea a millionaire," Bess said. "That'll show Tad."

On the stage one of the cat owners disappeared through an opening in the velvet backdrop.

"What's back there?" Nancy asked.

"There's a backstage area in all the galleries," George replied. "The exhibitors take their cats there before the showings for last-minute grooming."

The judge put the gray Manx back in its cage, went to another cage, and took out a white one.

"I think that's Cotton," Bess said excitedly. "I'm rooting for him."

The judge put Cotton on a table and studied him carefully. She then turned him over and rubbed his furry stomach. Cotton purred happily and tapped the judge's hand with his paw.

"What a good show cat," George commented. "Being handled like a ball of pizza dough doesn't seem to faze him one bit."

After she had seen all the Manx cats, the judge scribbled on a piece of paper, then pinned ribbons to the cages. The audience broke into applause.

"Cotton got a blue ribbon!" Bess cried.

"We must have brought him good luck," Nancy said, smiling. "I hope we can do the same for Purrfect."

"What do you mean?" George asked.

Nancy explained about the showing of long-haired breeds at four o'clock.

"Oh, Purrfect's a shoo-in," Bess declared with confidence. "All she has to do is bat those big green eyes at the judge."

"Come on," Nancy said, "let's go walk around some more until the showing."

Shortly before four o'clock the three girls made their way to gallery three.

"It's getting crowded in here. We'd better sit down, quick," Nancy said.

They found seats next to a plump woman in her late sixties. She wore a gold paisley dress and a green shawl, and her gray hair was tied back in a dainty chignon.

She regarded the girls curiously. "Hello, ladies," she said in a deep, crackly voice with a trace of a Southern accent. "Are you in the business?"

"The business?" Nancy repeated. "Oh, you mean the cat business? No, we're just spectators."

"That's nice," the woman said, nodding. "Nice that young people like cats. I'm Winona Bell."

The girls introduced themselves. "Are you in the business, Ms. Bell?" Bess asked her.

"Oh, yes. I used to be one of the top breeders in North Carolina. Won all the ribbons. Now I don't win so many ribbons. It's gotten to be a very crowded field."

17

"Are you one of the exhibitors at this show?" Nancy asked.

"Oh, sure," Winona said. "All short-haired cats, though."

"So you don't have any long-haired cats in this showing?" Bess said.

"I left all my long-haired cats back home. I don't have any good ones this year." Winona lowered her voice and smiled conspiratorially. "I almost did, though. I offered a young woman— what was her name, Annie? Her last name was something like Casey. Anyway, I offered her a great deal of money for her Persian. A beautiful Persian, silver-colored. But she wasn't interested in selling, she said."

"You mean Andrea Cassidy?" Bess offered.

"Yes, that's right, Andrea Cassidy," the older woman said. "I told her that—"

She paused, and her smile disappeared. She glanced nervously around the room. "Excuse me," she said hoarsely. "I'm not feeling well. I have to get a drink of water."

After she left, the girls exchanged a puzzled look.

"What was that all about?" Bess whispered.

"Who knows?" Nancy whispered back.

A few minutes later a heavyset man appeared on the stage. "Ladies and gentlemen," he said, "we're about to start the showing of long-haired breeds. Will you all take your seats, so that we can—"

18

Just then there was a scream from backstage, and Andrea came running out through the velvet backdrop. She dashed up to the heavyset man, waving her arms frantically.

"Somebody has stolen my cat!" she cried.

3

An Anonymous Note

The crowd gasped at Andrea's announcement. Then everyone began talking at once, adding to the atmosphere of chaos and confusion.

"Come on," Nancy said to her friends, jumping out of her seat. Within seconds she had made her way down the aisle and up onto the stage, where Andrea was conferring with the heavyset man and a middle-aged security guard. Bess and George followed at Nancy's heels.

Andrea saw them immediately. "Nancy, Bess, George, I'm so glad you're here. Someone has taken Purrfect!"

"What happened?" Nancy asked her.

"Oh, Nancy," Andrea said shakily, her brown eyes filling with tears. "I left her backstage for a few minutes in her portable carrier, and when I came back, the carrier was gone!"

"Ma'am?" the guard spoke up. "I've got the description of your cat, now I need a description of the carrier."

"It's about this big"—Andrea made a bread-box shape with her hands—"and off-white, with a black handle. There's a wire-mesh door at one end with a simple latch, no lock. Oh, and there's a square pink sticker on the side of it, with Purrfect's name along with my name and address."

The security guard took a walkie-talkie out of his pocket and began speaking into it. "Be on the alert for a cat carrier containing a three-year-old silver Persian with green eyes and a rhinestone collar. Believed to have been stolen from the backstage area of gallery three between three forty-five and three fifty-five. Terry and Fred, please split up and head immediately for the exits out of the backstage area. . . ."

Nancy leaned over to George and Bess. "Bess, go out into the main hall and try to find Tad Cassidy," she whispered. "George, you look for Winona Bell. One of them may have Purrfect."

"Winona Bell?" Bess repeated, a puzzled expression clouding her face. "You don't think—"

"Don't ask any questions, just go," Nancy said urgently. "And if they're on their way out the building, follow them."

Without waiting for a reply, Nancy headed backstage through the opening in the velvet backdrop.

The backstage area for gallery three was large

and crowded. About twenty-five to thirty cat owners and their assistants were standing around chattering nervously. There were card tables and folding chairs set up in the center of the room. On top of the tables were grooming tools, cans of powder, portable carriers, and a dozen or so long-haired cats preening, mostly Persians and Himalayans.

"Listen, everybody," Nancy said loudly. "A silver Persian named Purrfect is missing. She was in an off-white carrier with a black handle. Did any of you happen to notice her?"

"Sure," one woman said. "I know that cat. She's real pretty."

Nancy turned to her. "Did you see anyone handling her in the last half hour, or hanging around her carrier? Besides her owner, that is?"

The woman shrugged. "It's been crazy back here, with all of us trying to get our cats ready for the showing. There's no way any of us would have paid attention to that kind of thing." The other cat owners nodded in assent.

At that moment the security guard came backstage along with Andrea and the heavyset man. Andrea introduced him to Nancy as Mr. Angell, the judge for the long-haired showing.

"This incident is most unfortunate," Mr. Angell said. "Nothing like this has ever happened at this show."

"I've got my people searching the entire auditorium, as well as the parking lot," the guard said to Mr. Angell. He then pointed to two doors—one blue, one green—on opposite ends of the room. "I'm going to check out these exits."

"Fine, Karl," Mr. Angell said. "Ms. Cassidy, we've alerted the police, and they're going to want to ask you some questions. You should stay right here until they come."

"All right," Andrea said.

Nancy followed Karl as he headed for the blue door. "Where does that lead to?" Nancy asked.

"Down to the parking lot," he replied. "It's not used much, since most people who come in and out go through the main entrance, out front."

"Is it kept locked?"

Karl shook his head. "We keep all the exits open during normal business hours."

"How about the green door?" Nancy said. "Where does that go?"

"To the main hall of the auditorium."

"Is that the only place it leads to?" Nancy said. "Does it provide access to any of the other galleries, or their backstage areas?"

"Nope," Karl responded. "What is this, you want to be a security guard when you grow up or something?" He sounded amused.

Nancy grinned and said nothing.

They had reached the blue door. Karl grabbed the handle and jerked it open.

On the other side of it was a dimly lit stairwell. Nancy listened for any suspicious sounds but heard none.

"You can follow me down there, miss," Karl said. "But it's kind of dark, and you might get scared."

Nancy pulled a flashlight out of her purse and flicked it on. "I'll try to be brave," she said, smiling sweetly.

"Let's go," the guard said.

They closed the door behind them and started down. The air was cold and clammy, and there was a faint, mildewy smell.

Karl had turned his own flashlight on, and the two proceeded slowly, scanning for clues.

"A bunch of bulbs seem to be out," Karl noted. "I'd better tell the maintenance people."

They got to the door at the bottom of the stairs without finding anything. Just then the door was flung open, and Nancy was temporarily blinded by a powerful beam of light.

"Hold it right there!" a male voice rang out. "Oh, it's you, Karl. Sorry." The beam was averted.

Nancy blinked. There was a young security guard standing in the doorway, flashlight in hand. Beyond him was the parking lot.

"Hey, Fred," Karl said. "Any action?"

Fred shook his head. "I've been up and down these stairs, but no thief, and no cat. Terry's on the other exit, the one that leads out to the main hall. I just talked to him a second ago. Nothing happening there, either."

"Did anyone note any suspicious activity in the parking lot?" Nancy piped up.

Fred looked at her, then at Karl. "There are three men going through the lot. Nothing so far. And no cars have left in the last fifteen minutes."

"Great," Karl muttered. "I'm going to check on Terry, the other guard," he said to Nancy as they headed up the stairs.

Upstairs, Nancy found Andrea alone in the backstage area, pacing. Nancy noticed that George and Bess hadn't returned yet. "Were the police here already?" Nancy asked Andrea. "Did you talk to them?"

Andrea nodded. "Briefly. There's a policeman out in gallery three, questioning the other long-haired cat owners and their assistants. And there's more of them searching the auditorium." Her eyes welled up with fresh tears. "It's really hitting me now, seeing all these policemen and security guards running around. Purrfect is gone."

"They'll find her," Nancy said, wishing she could feel as sure as she sounded.

"But what if something happens to her?" Andrea said. "What if—"

"Whoever stole her knows she's a valuable cat," Nancy interrupted gently. "The thief isn't going to let any harm come to her."

Andrea was silent.

"Where did Mr. Angell go?" Nancy asked.

"He went off with the director of the cat show. They're going to get a flier going with a photograph of Purrfect." Andrea paused, looking agitated. "Nancy, you're a detective. Will you help me find Purrfect? I know the police and the security staff here will do everything they can, but I'd feel so much better knowing you were investigating, too."

"Of course I will," Nancy promised.

"Oh, thank you," Andrea said, hugging Nancy gratefully.

"Now that I'm officially on the case, I'll start off by asking you some questions," Nancy said. "You said that you left the backstage area for a few minutes, and when you came back, Purrfect was gone. How long were you away?"

"About ten minutes," Andrea said. "I had to go back to my booth to get some grooming tools. That was at three forty-five or so."

"So the thief could have had ten minutes to steal Purrfect," Nancy mused. "That would have been plenty of time to reach the parking lot through the blue door, even get in a car and drive off. But if the thief didn't get to Purrfect until, say, three fifty-four, which is only a minute or two before you returned and found Purrfect missing, he or she wouldn't have been able to leave the premises. Karl had guards posted at the exits and in the parking lot within seconds."

Andrea's eyes lit up. "You mean the thief could still be around here someplace? With Purrfect?"

"Maybe." Nancy paused for a moment. "Listen, Andrea. Before you went to get your grooming tools, did you happen to see anyone you knew hanging out backstage? Like Tad or Winona Bell?"

"No," Andrea replied, her expression growing troubled. "Nancy, you don't think Tad had anything to do with this? He may want Purrfect back very badly, but he would never resort to stealing her. He's not that kind of person."

Nancy wasn't so sure of Tad's innocence, especially in light of his earlier threat, but she didn't push the matter with Andrea. "What about Winona Bell, then?" Nancy asked.

"The funny old woman who wanted to buy Purrfect?" Andrea shrugged. "No, I didn't see her backstage. What makes you suspect—"

"Andrea, darling!"

Nancy turned to see a tall, attractive woman in her forties rushing toward them. She was dressed in a tangerine-colored suit, and her ebony-black hair was cut in a stylish pageboy. She wore flashy rhinestone earrings and a matching bracelet.

She placed a well-manicured hand on Andrea's arm. "Oh, darling, I heard about Purrfect. How dreadful. How absolutely, absolutely dreadful."

"Hello, Kara," Andrea said. "Nancy, this is Kara Kramer, from Simon-Ross Media. Kara, this is my friend Nancy Drew. Nancy is a de—"

"Pleased to meet you," Nancy cut in, smiling at Kara. She didn't want it spread around that she was investigating Purrfect's disappearance.

"Hello, Ms. Drew," Kara said, then turned to Andrea. "Darling, I'm just sick over this whole matter. That adorable kitty! And heaven knows what this will mean for our ad campaign."

27

"I know it," Andrea said. "But right now I just want Purrfect back, safe and sound."

"Well, of course, darling, of course. What's money compared to the life of a pet, and so forth. Listen, I'm late for an appointment." She squeezed Andrea's arm. "Call me if you hear anything, anything at all. I won't be able to sleep a wink until Purrfect is found."

"Is she in charge of the Kitty Classics ad campaign?" Nancy asked Andrea when Kara had left.

"That's right," Andrea replied. "She comes across as a bit theatrical, but underneath all that she's an extremely smart woman. She's done an incredible job with Purrfect's commercial."

"I may need to talk to her at some point. She might be able to help us," Nancy said.

"Just let me know when you want to see her. She's very busy, but I'll make sure you get an appointment right away." Andrea added, "After all, she has a stake in this, too."

"Oh, and Andrea?" Nancy said. "I need to keep a low profile while I'm on this case. So don't tell anyone I'm a detective, okay?"

"Sure thing," Andrea said. "I'm sorry I almost blurted it to Kara."

Two police officers appeared in the backstage area just then. "Ms. Cassidy?" one of them said. "Could we speak to you?"

"Sure," Andrea replied.

At that moment George and Bess rushed in. Nancy left Andrea's side and joined her friends.

"Well?" Nancy said in a low voice.

"No go," George said breathlessly. "I found Winona Bell's booth, but it was being manned by her assistant. He said that Winona wasn't feeling well, and she left around four o'clock."

Nancy's eyes gleamed. "Did he see her leave?"

"Nope. She called him from her hotel at about four-fifteen or so, saying she'd left and asking him to take over for the rest of the afternoon."

"I didn't do much better," Bess said, sighing. "No sign of Tad Cassidy anywhere. I even asked around, but no one could remember seeing him leave."

Andrea wandered over to them. The two policemen had left. "They're going through this auditorium with a fine-tooth comb. But so far, no thief, no Purrfect."

"Come on, we'll all do some combing ourselves," Nancy suggested. "It will make us feel better, and besides, you never know what four pairs of fresh eyes will find."

"Nothing like lemonade on a hot August day," George murmured appreciatively to Nancy and Bess.

The three girls had left Andrea at her car, then stopped by the Marvins' before going their separate ways. They sat in the kitchen, the cooling ice clinking in their lemonade glasses.

"As hot as it is outside, I'm glad I wore this thing," Nancy stated, patting the black linen jacket she wore over her white T-shirt and jeans.

29

"The air conditioning at the civic center was freezing. How about you, Bess? Weren't you cold in that thin blouse?"

Bess didn't reply. She was staring moodily off into space.

"Hello? Bess?" George tapped her cousin on the shoulder. "Earth to Bess. . . ."

"Oh, sorry." Bess focused her troubled blue eyes on George and Nancy. "I was just thinking about poor Purrfect. After all our searching, we didn't find a trace of her. And the police and the security guards didn't turn up anything, either. We're stuck at square one."

"I wouldn't say that we're at square *one*, exactly," Nancy said.

Bess leaned forward. "Why, Nancy Drew, are you holding out on us? What do you mean by that?"

Nancy shook her head, laughing. "I haven't solved the mystery yet, Bess. But I do have several theories."

"Like the Tad theory and the Winona theory," George said.

"Exactly," Nancy replied.

"I can see about Tad, especially after what he said to Andrea," Bess said. "But Winona? So Andrea wouldn't sell Purrfect to her. Could she have been that desperate?"

"It's something to consider, especially with her bolting out of gallery three right about the time Purrfect was stolen," Nancy said.

She paused to take a sip of lemonade. "I have

some other theories, though. First of all, Purrfect's kidnapping might have been the work of a prankster—someone trying to create a disturbance at the show. It could also have been a person, not Tad or Winona, who knows Purrfect's value and is planning to sell her or is hoping to collect ransom for her from Andrea."

"I just can't believe the thief was crazy enough to steal a cat right in the open," George muttered.

Nancy shrugged. "There were twenty-five or thirty people in that backstage area all rushing around, getting their cats ready. Who would have noticed someone picking up a cat carrier?"

"And you think the thief escaped through the blue door, the one that leads to the parking lot?" George asked.

"It seems likely," Nancy said. "The green door leads to the main hall. It wouldn't make sense to go all the way through the main hall if you're trying to get out of the civic center without getting caught."

"So what's next, Nan?" Bess queried.

Nancy finished off her lemonade. "First thing tomorrow we'll talk to Winona and Tad. Until then we'll just sleep on it."

By the time Nancy got home, it was nearly dinnertime. She stepped into the front hallway and heard the sounds of Hannah puttering in the kitchen.

"I'm home!" Nancy called out.

"Hi, Nancy! Dinner in ten minutes!" came Hannah's reply.

Nancy took off her linen jacket. "Hey, what's this?"

A piece of paper had fallen out of her jacket pocket. She bent down to pick it up.

It was a note, written in red ink:

Purrfect doesn't have nine lives, and neither do you. Stop your snooping, or it will be too late!

4

Bess's Discovery

"Where did *this* come from?" Nancy asked herself. She turned the note over in her hand. The paper was pale green with thin brown lines, and the top edge was perforated.

"Plain old stenography paper," Nancy concluded. "And the ink is from a common ballpoint pen."

She then studied the handwriting closely. The letters were large and childlike, as if the author had worked carefully to obscure his or her handwriting.

Nancy sat down in a chair and closed her eyes, trying to recapture the events of the afternoon. She remembered having her jacket on the entire time. So, at some point after Purrfect's disappearance, the thief had sneaked the note into her pocket—while she was wearing it! But when? And where? And how had the thief found out that she was working on the case?

After dinner Nancy drove over to Andrea's house, which was about ten minutes away. She found Andrea watching television in her living room.

"They just had a story about Purrfect on the local news," Andrea said forlornly after she offered Nancy a seat. "My poor little cat."

Nancy nodded sympathetically as she sat down on the couch. Then she pulled the note out of her purse. "I came to show you this. Someone slipped it into my pocket at the civic center."

Andrea read it quickly, then gasped. "This person sounds dangerous!" she cried. "What are we going to do?"

"As I said earlier, I don't think the thief is going to do anything to Purrfect," Nancy said reassuringly. "If any harm comes to her, she won't be worth as much. It's in the thief's best interests to keep her healthy and happy."

"I suppose so," Andrea murmured, turning off the television.

Nancy frowned. "I've been thinking. . . . This note tells me that the thief either returned to the scene of the crime after stealing Purrfect or stuck around the whole time. If the thief stayed in the civic center, it means that he or she might have had an accomplice take the cat away. Unless Purrfect was hidden somewhere at the show."

"An accomplice!" Andrea exclaimed. "Are you saying that there could be more than one criminal with his hands on my cat?"

"Maybe," Nancy said.

"Oh, this is terrible." Andrea moaned. "What now? Are you going to do what the note says and stop looking for Purrfect altogether? After all, you could be in danger."

"Oh, no, just the opposite," Nancy insisted. "I think I should look for her twice as hard. We're obviously dealing with a nasty character, and the sooner we get Purrfect back, the better."

"Do you have a plan?" Andrea asked.

"I'd like to talk to a few people tomorrow," Nancy said. "One of them is Winona Bell. When did she first contact you about buying Purrfect?"

"She called me a few days ago," Andrea responded. "She'd just gotten into town for the show. She was very pushy about Purrfect—she offered me a lot of money for her—but I was adamant about not selling her, so she finally gave up. She approached me once more at the show, on opening day, but I told her I hadn't changed my mind, and that was that."

"How did she know about Purrfect?" Nancy asked. "You said that this is Purrfect's first major competition, right?"

"The cat-breeding world is very small," Andrea explained. "Purrfect *has* been in a few not-so-major shows, and, well, word gets around about who's got the best-looking Persians. And of course, there is the commercial. Even though it hasn't aired yet, there's been gossip about it."

Nancy was silent for a moment. Finally she said, "The other person I want to speak to tomorrow is Tad."

"Tad?" Andrea repeated. "But I told you—"

"I know you don't think he had anything to do with Purrfect's kidnapping," Nancy said gently. "But he did threaten to take her away from you just a few hours before she disappeared."

"I see your point," Andrea conceded. "In that case, I'll tell you where you can catch up with him."

"Will I see you at the show tomorrow?" Nancy asked as she got up to leave.

"I may be there briefly," Andrea replied. "There's not much for me to do there, with Purrfect gone. I thought I'd spend the next few days posting fliers around town, maybe putting ads in local and national newspapers."

"Sounds like a good idea," Nancy said enthusiastically. "Every little thing we can do to find Purrfect will help."

The next morning Nancy and Bess found themselves in Taste Temptations, Tad's gourmet food store in downtown River Heights. George had a tennis date but had promised to check in with them later. The shop was a stylishly decorated place, with a black and white tiled floor, a high ceiling, and white brick walls adorned with photographs of beautifully arranged foods. There were several aisles of exotic-looking merchandise, and a few tables in the corner that served as a café.

A young, dark-haired woman appeared from behind the counter. She was dressed in a short black skirt and a white T-shirt. "Can I help you ladies?" she said cheerfully.

"Is Tad Cassidy here?" Nancy asked her.

The young woman glanced at a closed door. "He's in his office, talking on the phone. As soon as he's off, I'll get him for you. In the meantime, feel free to look around."

The girls thanked her.

"Wow!" Bess exclaimed, pointing at a display of lavishly decorated cakes. "Have you ever seen anything like that?"

Nancy glanced at Tad's door. "Listen, Bess," she whispered. "Go occupy the clerk at the other end of the store. Ask her some questions about something, anything."

"Okay, boss," Bess whispered back.

A second later Nancy was standing at a shelf near Tad's office, pretending to be engrossed in a box of spinach fettuccini. She could hear his voice coming through the door, very faintly.

"I need more time. I know the loan payment is due now, but——" There was a long silence.

Nancy was hoping to hear more when the door suddenly opened. Tad emerged, a troubled expression clouding his face.

When he caught sight of Nancy, he put on a smile and came toward her. "Hi, can I help you with—"

Then a flash of recognition crossed his face, and his smile grew cool. "Oh, it's *you*. What do you want?"

"I'd like to ask you some questions about Purrfect," Nancy replied.

Tad folded his arms across his chest. "I'd like to play twenty questions with you, but as you can see, I have a business to run. So if you'll just be on your way—"

"Where were you yesterday around four o'clock, when Purrfect disappeared?" Nancy interrupted smoothly.

"What are you saying, that I had something to do with that?" Tad said incredulously.

"I overheard your conversation with Andrea," Nancy told him. "You threatened to take Purrfect away from her."

"Look here, Ms. Drew," Tad said, "you don't know the whole story about that. And I'm a little tired of standing here listening to your accusations."

"I haven't accused you of anything," Nancy countered. "I'm simply trying to help Andrea find her cat. She's my friend."

"Look, I'm as upset about Purrfect's disappearance as she is. When I heard about it on the news last night, I felt sick." Tad paused. "But I'm sure you realize that Purrfect is a very special, very valuable cat—especially now that she's

38

going to be in a commercial. Any one of the hundreds of people at the show yesterday could have had the motive, and the opportunity, to kidnap her. Particularly the opportunity—there's no real security in the place. It's such a madhouse a person could steal an elephant out of there and nobody would notice."

"Why were you at the show, anyway?" Nancy asked. "Are you an exhibitor?"

Tad groaned. "More questions. I like cats, all right? I'm on the board of the local cat shelter, and I attend any events having to do with cats. Satisfied?"

"How did you find out about the commercial?"

Tad shrugged. "I ran into my friend Laura yesterday, and she told me. She's the one who introduced Andrea to Kara Kramer at the ad agency."

The young clerk came up to him just then and whispered something in his ear. Tad nodded, then turned to Nancy.

"This little interrogation is going to have to come to an end," he said gruffly. "I have some business to take care of."

He went over to a customer standing at the counter. Nancy found Bess at the other end of the store, looking at a tin of tea.

"Let's go, Bess," Nancy said. "We've got a lot of work to do."

On the way to the civic center Nancy filled in Bess on her conversation with Tad.

"He's not exactly Prince Charming, is he?" Bess remarked.

"You're telling me," Nancy murmured.

Bess studied her nails, then said, "Either his attitude means that he's hiding something, or it's just his personality. Which do you think it is, Nan?"

"I don't know," Nancy said thoughtfully. "And there's the thing about the loan payment," she continued. "I'll have to ask Andrea about that. If it turns out that he's having money problems, well, that might just send him to the top of my suspect list."

When the girls got to the civic center, they found Andrea cleaning up her booth.

"I just stopped by for a moment to straighten things up," Andrea said. "You know, to get the booth ready for when Purrfect comes back." Andrea picked up a pink ball and looked at it forlornly. "Purrfect's favorite toy. I wonder if she misses it."

"Have you heard anything from the police?" Nancy asked her.

"I just spoke to them a few minutes ago," Andrea replied. "They haven't got any leads, but they're working on it, they said. They're interviewing all the exhibitors and staff people here." She paused. "Did you talk to Tad?"

"He wasn't terribly helpful," Nancy said. "Tell me, Andrea, do you know whether or not he's in good shape financially?"

Andrea frowned. "You mean with Taste Temptations? It's been up and down. He did a big renovation on the store recently, though, and I think that's helped."

"Did he get a loan to do the renovation?" Nancy asked.

"Yes," Andrea replied. "Why all the questions about Tad's finances?"

"Just wondering." Nancy glanced at her watch. "Listen, Andrea, Bess and I have a few things to do here. We'll catch up with you a little later."

"I'm going to head out in a few minutes," Andrea told her. "Call me at home if you find anything."

Nancy and Bess waved goodbye and made their way up the busy aisle.

"It's just as crowded as it was yesterday," Nancy remarked after several people bumped into her. "Now I understand how the thief slipped that note into my pocket. With all this jostling, I would never have noticed."

"It's pretty crazy, all right," Bess agreed. "Well, what do we do next?"

"Let's go over to the information booth and see where Winona Bell's booth is," Nancy suggested. "I want to talk to her."

The information clerk had a list of all the exhibitors on a computer printout. "Bell, Bell . . . let's see here. Oh, yes, Ms. Bell has booth forty-two A."

"Where is that?" Nancy asked.

The clerk pointed to an area near the far side of the main hall. "The forties are all in that direction. You shouldn't have any problem finding her."

"Thank you," Nancy said.

"Listen, Nan, I'm going to get a soda and then catch up with you," Bess said. "Do you want anything?"

Nancy shook her head. "I'll see you at forty-two A."

"Be there in a jiffy," Bess promised.

Nancy headed briskly down an aisle. Just then she spotted a familiar figure out of the corner of her eye.

It was Winona Bell, standing in front of an unmanned booth. She seemed to be very interested in a cat inside one of the cages.

Nancy stepped behind another booth and watched. Winona glanced around furtively, then began scribbling something in a notebook.

After a few minutes Winona scurried back to her booth. Nancy went up to where she'd been and peeked inside the cage. Inside was a beautiful caramel-colored cat with long, luxurious fur.

"A Persian," Nancy said to herself. She waited a moment, then walked toward Winona as casually as possible, pretending to study some other booths along the way.

Winona's booth was a small one, with several cages of short-haired cats. When Nancy reached it, the old woman was sitting in a folding chair, looking slightly pink and out of breath.

"Hello, Ms. Bell," Nancy said. "I'm Nancy

Drew. Do you remember me? We met yesterday afternoon in gallery three."

Winona squinted at Nancy. "Oh, it's you. Hello, young lady. Where're your friends?"

"One of them is here. She's getting something to drink. The other one had a tennis date," Nancy explained.

"Tennis, oh, dear. Too much running around, if you ask me," Winona muttered. "Do you like my cats?"

Nancy moved closer to the cages. "Very pretty. What kind are they?"

Winona pointed to a pale silver cat with black spots. "This is Nefertiti, an Egyptian mau."

"She's beautiful," Nancy remarked.

"And this is Mr. Peabody, my Abyssinian." Winona indicated a copper-colored cat.

"No long-haired cats?" Nancy inquired innocently.

"No, no long-haireds," Winona replied. "I think I mentioned to you yesterday that I only brought up my short-haireds."

"That's right, I'd forgotten." Nancy smiled. "By the way, are you feeling better today?"

Winona looked confused. "What?"

"You weren't feeling well yesterday. You had to rush off to the drinking fountain," Nancy reminded Winona, watching her closely.

Winona's eyes widened. "Oh, yes, yes, I'm feeling fine now. It was just a little thing I get now and then—"

43

"Nancy!"

Bess rushed toward them. "Nancy, I've got to talk to you right away."

"Excuse me," Nancy said to Winona.

Nancy and Bess moved a little way down the aisle, out of Winona's earshot.

"What's up?" Nancy said in a low voice.

"Nancy, you'll never believe it!" Bess cried excitedly. "I've just found Purrfect!"

5

Two of a Kind

"You've *what?*" Nancy burst out.

Bess grabbed Nancy's hand. "No time to explain. Come on, I'll show you."

Bess led her friend through the crowd, and a few minutes later the girls were standing in front of an unmanned booth with several lavishly decorated cages.

"The cage on the left," Bess said triumphantly. "Purrfect herself, in the flesh!"

Nancy bent down and looked inside. A large silver Persian lay curled up in a ball, sleeping.

Nancy whistled. "That sure looks like Purrfect, doesn't it?" She glanced around. "I want to get this cage open and take a closer look. Bess, make sure no one sees me. I'll try to be quick."

Just as Nancy was reaching for the latch, however, the Persian woke up. She studied the two strangers warily.

"Whoops," Nancy said, frowning. "Bess, this isn't Purrfect."

"What do you mean?" Bess cried.

"This cat has blue eyes. Purrfect has green eyes," Nancy explained. "Otherwise, they look completely identical. This cat even has the same rhinestone collar."

"*A-hem.*"

Nancy and Bess peered over their shoulders. Nancy recognized the fair-haired man with a thin mustache from the previous day. The cat breeder Sean Dunleavy regarded them suspiciously. His hands were stuffed in the pockets of his brown corduroy slacks.

"May I help you with something, ladies?" he asked in a British accent.

"We were just looking at your cat," Nancy replied, smiling.

"Obviously," Sean murmured, not returning her smile. "Did my assistant give you permission to open this cage?"

"Your assistant?" Nancy echoed. "No, actually, there wasn't anyone here."

Sean nodded. "Oh, but of course. You waited until she stepped away, so that it would be easier for you to steal Desdemona."

"Steal Desdemona? You mean this cat?" Bess shook her head. "No, you've got it all wrong."

"Why don't we go over to the security office,

and you can tell your story to the authorities," Sean said crisply.

Nancy felt herself flushing with anger. "Look, Mr. Dunleavy, I'm sorry we started to open this cage without your permission, but we had a good reason." She went on to explain the mix-up.

"Anybody who knows anything could tell the difference between the two cats," Sean scoffed. "Desdemona is clearly a superior cat. Why, just look at her form!"

Nancy frowned thoughtfully. "Was Desdemona entered in the showing of long-haired breeds?"

"Yes," Sean replied, shrugging. "She took first place, of course."

"Then why weren't you in the backstage area when Purrfect disappeared?" Nancy inquired.

"Listen, Ms.—what did you say your name was?"

"Drew," Nancy replied. "Nancy Drew. And this is my friend Bess Marvin."

"Nancy is helping Andrea Cassidy find Purrfect," Bess interjected.

Sean waved his hands impatiently and turned to Nancy. "My assistant and I were extremely late getting to the show due to some problems with our flight."

Nancy nodded. Yesterday, when she and the girls had been at Andrea's booth, they had overheard Sean yelling about customs officials.

"We spent most of yesterday afternoon running

around, getting registered, setting up, and so forth," Sean continued. "We didn't get to gallery three until four-thirty, but as it turned out, the showing was delayed until early this morning, due to this cat-theft business."

"I see," Nancy said.

"With a cat thief around who is fond of Persians, you can understand why I wasn't terribly happy to see you two young ladies hovering around Desdemona's cage," Sean continued. "Since the incident yesterday I've been very careful with all my cats, especially Desdemona. I even asked Gillian to make sure that—where is that girl, anyway?"

"Gillian is your assistant?" Nancy asked him.

"Yes, when she's not taking one of her extraordinarily long breaks," Sean said sarcastically.

Desdemona began meowing loudly.

Sean glanced at her. "Time for your lunch, eh, Desdemona? Look, Ms. Drew, you and your friend are going to have to excuse me now. I've enjoyed our chat ever so much, but I have things to do."

Bess said to Nancy as they walked away, "He's got a wee little ego problem, doesn't he?"

"Yup," Nancy agreed, chuckling.

"I'm sorry I got us into that," Bess apologized. "It wouldn't have happened if I hadn't confused the two cats."

"Desdemona had me fooled, too, until she opened her eyes," Nancy said. "Besides, I'm glad we got a chance to meet Mr. Dunleavy. He may be useful to us in our investigation."

The two girls stopped at the refreshment stand for a late lunch. "Order me something, okay, Bess?" Nancy said. "I want to call Andrea."

Nancy found the phone booth and dialed Andrea's number. Andrea answered on the eighth ring, sounding out of breath.

"Hello?"

"Andrea, this is Nancy."

"Oh, hi! I just got in the door. Any news?"

"Nothing too exciting," Nancy replied. "Listen, can you get me an appointment with Kara Kramer at Simon-Ross Media as soon as possible? Maybe tomorrow?"

"No problem. I'll call her right away." Andrea paused. "Speaking of tomorrow, I forgot to mention to you—the cat show people are sponsoring a big fund-raising dance at the River Heights Country Club tomorrow night. I'd like you and Bess and George to come with me as my guests. It should be fun, and besides, everyone involved with the show will be there. It'll be a good time to scout them out."

"Sounds great," Nancy said eagerly.

After promising to call her later that day, Nancy went back to the refreshment stand. Bess was sitting at a small table with a tray full of food.

"Here we go. Spaghetti and meatballs for two," Bess announced cheerfully.

"Yum," Nancy said.

49

As they ate, Nancy and Bess discussed the case.

"Oh, I forgot to tell you," Nancy said suddenly. "Andrea's invited us to the country club tomorrow night. The cat show people are sponsoring a big fund-raising dance."

"Great!" Bess exclaimed. "I have a new dress I've been dying to wear. It's pale blue, and it has—"

She was interrupted just then by a soft English voice. "Excuse me."

A young woman was hovering by their table. She had shoulder-length, curly brown hair, a small face covered with freckles, and hazel eyes. She was wearing a lilac-colored T-shirt and jeans. Nancy recognized her at once as the woman Sean had been yelling at yesterday.

"I'm sorry to bother you," the woman murmured. "I'm Gillian Samms. I work as an assistant for Sean Dunleavy, one of the exhibitors."

Nancy and Bess introduced themselves.

"We actually met Mr. Dunleavy just a few minutes ago," Nancy said.

Gillian regarded Nancy anxiously. "You're the detective, right? The detective who's investigating that cat's disappearance?"

Nancy frowned. "Who told you that?"

"I—I overheard one of the security guards talking about you. He said that you're a famous detective, and that you were following one of the other guards around yesterday looking for the cat." Gillian blushed. "I'm sorry, am I not supposed to know?"

Nancy didn't want people to find out that she was investigating Purrfect's case, but there was nothing she could do about Gillian's knowing.

"Don't worry about it," she said finally. "So, what can we do for you?"

"I have something important to tell you," Gillian said. "Something that might help you find Ms. Cassidy's cat."

"Please sit down," Nancy said.

Gillian glanced around quickly, then joined the two girls. "I shouldn't be doing this," she said in a low voice. "Sean will be very angry if he finds out."

"Your boss doesn't seem like the most pleasant person in the world to work for," Bess said sympathetically.

Gillian's eyes lit up. "Oh, I'm glad you said that. I sometimes think it's all in my head, that it's my fault I don't get along better with him, but the truth is that he's . . . well, the truth is, I'm frightened of him."

"Frightened of him?" Nancy repeated. "Why?"

"He's got the most horrible temper," Gillian explained. "He's always screaming at me about something, always blaming me for things. He has a great, driving need to be the best in his field, and if anything interferes with that, any little thing, well, it makes him crazy."

"Why don't you just quit, then?" Bess asked her. "There must be other cat breeders you could work for."

Gillian shook her head. "I'm brand new in the field. I should actually consider myself lucky to have a job at all, much less a job with someone as prominent as Sean."

"You said you had some information about Purrfect?" Nancy prompted.

"That's right," Gillian said. "You see, I think Sean may have taken her."

"What!" Nancy exclaimed.

Gillian nodded. "A little before four o'clock yesterday I had a quick question to ask him. So I went to the registration booth, where he was supposed to be filling out forms. But he wasn't there."

"Maybe he had finished by the time you got there," Nancy suggested.

"I asked the registration clerk. She said that Sean was halfway through the forms when he told her that he had something urgent to take care of and disappeared."

"That does sound a little suspicious," Bess agreed. "Purrfect was stolen right before four, right?"

"But why would he want to steal Purrfect?" Nancy asked.

"Desdemona is his big prize cat this year, and he was counting on her to sweep this show," Gillian said. "But a few weeks ago he found out about Purrfect. You see, Desdemona and Purrfect are very similar."

"You can say that again," Bess muttered.

"Are you saying that Sean Dunleavy may have

stolen Purrfect to eliminate the competition?" Nancy said incredulously.

Gillian nodded. "You see, there was an incident, about a year ago, when—"

"Gillian!"

The three girls whirled around. Sean Dunleavy was standing just a few feet away. And the hard scowl on his face told them that he was not in a happy mood.

6

A Visit with Kara Kramer

Gillian turned white. "I'm sorry, Sean, I was just—"

"She was just having some lunch with us," Nancy interjected.

Sean tapped his watch impatiently. "Gillian, you're supposed to be at the booth. Every time I turn around, you're off someplace."

"We apologize for keeping Gillian, but she had so many stories to tell about all the shows you've won," Bess said, smiling sweetly.

Sean glowered at Gillian and took her arm. "Come along, Gillian. We have work to do."

"I'll talk to you later," Gillian whispered to Nancy as she rose from the table.

When the cat breeder and his assistant had gone, Bess clamped a hand to her forehead. "Whew, that was close!"

"Maybe closer than we think," Nancy murmured. "I wonder if he heard what Gillian was saying?"

"I think he was just mad about Gillian hanging out with us," Bess said.

"I hope so, Bess." Nancy frowned. "I wish I knew what Gillian was trying to tell us. She said something about an incident."

"It sounded juicy, whatever it was," Bess remarked, finishing off her spaghetti.

Nancy dabbed at her lips with a paper napkin and stood up. "Come on, Bess. Let's swing by Sean's booth before we leave. Maybe we can catch Gillian alone."

But when the girls reached Sean's aisle, they could see that the English cat breeder was busy barking orders at Gillian.

"Oh, well," Nancy said, disappointed. "I'll have to try again later."

"Why don't you call her?" Bess suggested.

Nancy shook her head. "I don't know where she and Sean are staying, and I don't want to call attention to ourselves by trying to find out. Sean is suspicious of us as it is. Besides, if I can't get her alone here, I can always talk to her at the dance tomorrow. I bet they'll be there."

The offices of Simon-Ross Media were located in downtown River Heights. On Wednesday afternoon Nancy, Bess, and George walked into the reception area and were told to have a seat.

"Ms. Kramer is in conference right now, but

she should be through in just a few minutes," the receptionist informed them.

On the coffee table was a terra-cotta pot filled with fresh flowers and a dozen magazines arranged in a fan.

Bess picked a magazine up and squinted at the cover, which featured a woman in a yellow vinyl dress. "Wow! This is what they wear in, in— where is this magazine from, Italy?"

"Spain," Nancy said. "I think that's what the models wear. You probably wouldn't see that dress on the average Spanish woman walking down the street."

"It looks totally impractical," George observed. "I mean, how could you move in it? It's skin-tight down to the ankles."

"Oh, George, where's your imagination, your sense of drama?" Bess replied.

"I wonder how much longer Kara Kramer is going to be?" Nancy murmured.

"What are you hoping to find out from her, anyway?" George asked with a grin. "Are you thinking that maybe Kitty Classics' main rival, Fussy Felines, abducted Purrfect to weaken the competition?"

Nancy chuckled. "Interesting theory. Actually, what I was thinking of was—"

Just then Kara Kramer swept into the reception area, a legal pad tucked under one arm. She wore an indigo blue dress with matching pumps and red earrings that contrasted with her black hair.

"I thought that tedious meeting would never end," she said breathlessly. "Come with me, ladies."

They followed her through a long hallway lined with cubicles. Dozens of men and women sat in front of computers, punching keys.

"Right here," Kara said, pointing to a half-open door. "Excuse the mess. We're right in the middle of the Kitty Classics campaign, and well, things have been quite hectic."

The three girls found themselves in a large office. When they were all seated, Kara folded her manicured hands together tightly and said, "Now, what can I do for you? Andrea Cassidy said that you wanted to see me, but she didn't go into details."

"I'd like to ask you some questions about Purrfect," Nancy said. "I thought that you might be able to tell me a little about the Kitty Classics campaign."

"Are you doing an article on the campaign?" Kara asked.

Nancy shook her head. She tried to think of a way to avoid telling Kara that she was a detective.

"No, I'm not writing an article," Nancy replied after a moment. "Andrea is a friend, and we're all trying to help her out."

"Help her out? You mean, find out what happened to her cat?" Kara said.

"That's right," Nancy replied.

Kara raised one eyebrow. "Why, Ms. Drew.

You're not thinking that any of us at Simon-Ross Media had anything to do with Purrfect's kidnapping, are you?"

"I'd like to get as much information on Purrfect as possible," Nancy explained. "Whoever stole her was aware of her value, which means that he or she might have known about the commercial."

"And you're suggesting that maybe someone here leaked the news that Purrfect was a hot star in the making?" Kara finished.

"Something like that," Nancy replied.

"How suspicious you are," Kara declared, her voice full of amusement. "Let me tell you ladies a little something about the advertising business. It's bad, very bad indeed, to leak information about a commercial before it airs. It ruins the surprise element, which is so terribly *vital* in getting the viewer's attention."

"But according to Andrea, several people at the cat show knew about Purrfect's commercial," Nancy said, frowning.

"That didn't come from anyone in this company," Kara retorted. "The people who work for me are absolutely trustworthy. They know better than to divulge company secrets. It was probably Andrea's friend who introduced her to me—what is her name, Laura Murphy?"

"I see," Nancy said, nodding thoughtfully. "I have another question. Can you think of anyone who might have wanted to kidnap Purrfect to make life difficult for you, or for Simon-Ross Media?"

"Make life *difficult?* But you don't understand . . ." Kara hesitated.

"Yes?" Nancy prompted.

Kara brushed back a lock of shiny black hair
and smiled nervously. "What I meant to say was,
the commercial has already been shot. Of course
we'll want Purrfect for future commercials, but I
trust that when that time comes she will have
been found."

Just then there was a knock on the door.

Kara groaned. "Yes, what is it?"

A young man peeked in. He was tall and
handsome, with wavy auburn hair and blue
eyes.

"Sorry to bother you," he said. "McGuffey is
here, and he needs your input on something."

"Thanks, Neal." Kara rose from her desk.
"This will just take five minutes."

When she had left, George turned to Nancy.
"Well? This isn't getting us very far, is it?"

"I wouldn't say that, exactly," Nancy replied.

"What do you mean, Nan?" Bess asked.

"When I asked Kara whether anybody might
have wanted to kidnap Purrfect to make trouble
for her or the company—she started to say
something else, then changed her mind," Nancy
recounted.

"What do you think she was starting to say?"
George asked.

"I'm not sure," Nancy said, standing up. "But
I'm going to see if I can find out."

Keeping one eye on the door, she walked
casually to Kara's desk. Carefully she began

59

sifting through the clutter on top, which consisted of a cup of lukewarm tea, an appointment book, piles of correspondence, and a couple of artist's sketches.

"Nancy, you're making me nervous," Bess whispered. "What if that cute guy walks in here again?"

"If he does, you can pretend to have a fainting spell and fall into his arms," George teased. "That will distract him long enough for Nancy to get back into her chair."

Bess stood up and headed for the door. "The suspense is too much for me. I'm going to go get a drink of water."

After a moment Nancy held up a piece of paper. "Here we go!"

"What have you got?" George asked.

"It's a file copy of a memo from Kara to the president of Simon-Ross Media, Matthew Sweeney."

"And?" George prompted.

Nancy's eyes were sparkling. "Listen to this. It says, 'The publicity generated by Purrfect's kidnapping should ensure the success of the Kitty Classics campaign. I propose to go through every available PR channel to see that the story is covered not just locally but nationally, in magazines, newspapers, and TV news shows.'"

George gasped. "What?"

"Not only that. This memo is dated Monday, the day Purrfect was stolen."

"Kara didn't waste any time," George remarked dryly. "So she's not upset that Purrfect is gone. She's actually *glad*."

"Or worse," Nancy said slowly. "Maybe Kara Kramer engineered Purrfect's disappearance in the first place!"

7

Ambushed!

Just then Nancy and George heard footsteps coming down the hall.

"Nan!" George whispered, gesturing toward the door.

Nancy smoothly returned the memo to its place on Kara's desk. When Kara walked in two seconds later, Nancy was standing across the room admiring an advertising poster.

"So sorry," Kara murmured. "Clients, you know."

"Lovely poster," Nancy remarked.

"Oh, yes, Pavel perfume. One of my first accounts. A raging success, if I do say so myself. It was my idea to use the . . ." Kara paused and looked around. "Weren't there three of you?"

At that moment Bess came through the door. "I

went for a drink," she explained, then glanced meaningfully at Nancy and George. "I hope I didn't miss anything."

"No," Nancy replied. "In fact, Ms. Kramer, we should be going. We've taken up enough of your time."

"Oh, no, I'm ever so glad to be of help." Kara placed a hand on Nancy's elbow. "Do let me know if there's anything more I can do to help dear Andrea. *Such* a dreadful situation for her."

"I'll be in touch," Nancy promised.

As soon as they got outside the Simon-Ross Media building, Nancy filled Bess in on the memo.

"So you think Kara Kramer could have done it?" Bess said.

"She was at the cat show Monday," Nancy replied. "She could have abducted Purrfect, taken her out to the parking lot to her car, then come back through the front entrance. It was about four-fifteen or so when she showed up in the backstage area to talk to Andrea. And afterward, she was in an awful hurry to get out of there."

"Having a stolen cat in her car would explain that," George remarked. "Well, Bess? While you were hiding at the drinking fountain, Nancy was solving the mystery."

Nancy laughed. "This mystery isn't solved yet, George. After all, that memo isn't any sort of proof that Kara is our kidnapper. It simply gives her a motive."

"That's right, George," Bess said. "Besides, while you two were playing spy, I was doing a little detective work of my own."

"What do you mean?" Nancy asked.

"Well, when I went off to get a drink, guess who I happened to run into?" Bess asked excitedly. "That guy, Neal Grant! You know, the one who poked his head into Kara's office? It turns out that he's her assistant. We had a nice long talk, and I think he could be a very useful source of information about Kara and the company."

Nancy and George exchanged a quick, amused glance.

"Hey, I'm serious!" Bess protested. "I mean, so what if he's gorgeous? This is business."

"You have a point, Bess," Nancy agreed. "It's going to take some work to prove anything on Kara."

Nancy glanced at her watch and said, "Hey, it's five o'clock. Maybe we should be thinking about going home and getting ready for the dance."

"Five o'clock!" Bess exclaimed. "I had no idea it was so late. I'll never be able to get ready in time!" She started race-walking to the parking lot.

Nancy and George followed her. "You've only got three hours to throw on a dress and run a comb through your hair, but maybe you'll pull it off somehow," George called out.

"George!" Bess protested.

While the cousins continued their bantering,

Nancy's thoughts returned to the case. Tad, Winona, Sean, Kara—did one of them have Purrfect? Or was it someone else entirely? Each of the four had had the motive and the opportunity. But Nancy couldn't shake the feeling that she was missing some angle. And her instincts told her that it was the key to the whole mystery.

At eight o'clock Nancy, Bess, and George arrived at the River Heights Country Club.

"You two look great," Nancy declared as she handed her car keys to a valet. Bess was wearing a pale blue dress with lavender trim and a big lavender bow at the waist. George's dress was made of dark green velvet. Its sleeveless, form-fitting style complemented her tall, slim figure.

"Speak for yourself, Nan," Bess said. "What a fantastic dress."

Nancy wore a white, off-the-shoulder dress with a full skirt that consisted of many layers of wispy chiffon. A pearl necklace and matching bracelet completed the outfit.

"Hi, girls!" Andrea was rushing up to them, waving a silver evening bag. "I'm sorry I'm late. I was on the phone with the police."

"Do they have any news?" Nancy asked eagerly.

"No. They said that they're working on it, though." Andrea paused. "Of course, that's what they've been saying for the last three days." She hung her head, and Nancy noticed that her eyes had filled with tears.

"Come on, Andrea," Nancy said gently, putting her arm around the young woman's shoulders. "We're going to find Purrfect real soon. In the meantime, let's have some fun. There's nothing like a party to lift the spirits."

As they entered the lobby, they could hear the strains of a lively dance band. Men in tuxedos and women in elegant dresses drifted by, talking and laughing.

Andrea began to cheer up slightly. "You're right, Nancy. This is just what I needed to get my mind off things."

They checked their wraps and found the ballroom. It was enormous, with high ceilings, tall windows, and a marble floor. Hundreds of white candles cast a warm, intimate glow through the ballroom. Several sets of graceful French doors led onto a terrace. The river glimmered beyond.

"What a crowd," George remarked. "I wonder who all is here?"

Nancy looked out over the dance floor, where a number of people were enjoying the band. There were also many guests standing on the sidelines. She noted Kara, Neal, Sean, Gillian, Winona, and Tad among them. Nancy was especially glad to see Gillian present. She was eager to finish their conversation from yesterday.

"Doesn't Neal look handsome?" Bess sighed. "And look at that thing Kara is wearing. Isn't it too cool?"

Kara was holding court with Neal and two other men. She had on a strapless silver gown, long black gloves, and a slender diamond necklace. She seemed to be dominating the small group's conversation, gesturing dramatically with an empty champagne glass as she talked.

"It's very Kara," George remarked with a grin.

Bess turned to the others. "I'm going to try to find a buffet table or something. I was so busy getting dressed, I didn't get much dinner."

"I think I'll wander around a bit myself," Nancy said to Andrea and George. "Excuse me."

As Nancy walked away, she heard George whisper to Andrea, "Translation—she's going to do some sleuthing."

Chuckling to herself, Nancy made her way through the crowd. She headed in Gillian's direction, but then saw that Sean was by her side, talking animatedly.

Rats, Nancy thought. He doesn't look as though he's going anywhere, either. How am I going to get Gillian alone?

"Punch?"

Nancy turned around. She'd somehow ended up next to the punch table, and a man was extending a cup to her. On his tuxedo lapel was a name tag that read, J. Reese, Director, Great Midwestern Cat Show.

"Oh, thank you, yes." Nancy smiled. "I'm pleased to meet you, Mr. Reese. I'm Nancy Drew. I'm a friend of Andrea Cassidy."

"You're helping to find the missing Persian," Mr. Reese said, nodding sadly. "It's terrible, what happened. Never in the history of this show has there been such a scandal. The national and local press are having a field day with it, and the publicity is killing us. All the criticism about our security—why, no one will ever want to enter their cats in our show again."

Nancy was silent, remembering Kara's memo to her boss. Without Kara Kramer, the publicity wouldn't be nearly so extensive, she thought.

"As it is, many of the exhibitors have been threatening to withdraw from the show," Mr. Reese continued. "They're all afraid that this cat thief will get their cats next."

"What a shame," Nancy said. "It's such a wonderful show. A lot of interesting cats, and interesting cat owners, too. I've met several of them in the last few days. Sean Dunleavy, for instance. And Winona Bell."

"Oh, yes. I know them both," Mr. Reese said. "Winona Bell is a nice lady. Too bad about her health—if it weren't for that, she'd still be one of the best in her field."

Nancy raised her eyebrows. "Her health?"

"She developed some sort of heart condition a few years ago. Nothing serious or life-threatening, but she tires easily, gets dizzy spells now and then. Recently it's kept her from traveling to a lot of the big shows." Mr. Reese sipped his punch. "Why, she had one of her spells just the other day. I had to help her find a cab so that she could get back to her hotel room and rest."

"When was this, exactly?" Nancy asked.

Mr. Reese squinted thoughtfully. "Let's see, it

was the first day of the show. Monday. That's right, Monday, just before four o'clock. I found her at a drinking fountain near gallery three, looking rather faint."

Nancy's mind raced. Did that mean Winona was off the hook as far as Purrfect was concerned? Or could she have been faking a spell in order to sneak Purrfect out of the civic center without arousing suspicion?

"I'm sure Winona was glad for your help," Nancy said smoothly. "Especially since she was carrying such a load."

"What do you mean?" Mr. Reese asked quizzically.

"Well, just before four I saw her in gallery three with a big cat carrier in her hand. It looked awfully heavy, and I'm sure it wasn't helping her condition any," Nancy replied.

"She didn't have it with her when I saw her," Mr. Reese said, looking puzzled. "She wasn't carrying anything, in fact—just a small purse, I believe."

Just then a young blond woman approached Mr. Reese and told him he had a call.

He turned to Nancy. "Excuse me, Ms. Drew. It was nice talking to you. I hope your friend finds her cat soon."

"So do I," Nancy said. Sipping her punch, she thought about what Mr. Reese had said. Could Winona have somehow gone backstage that day, taken Purrfect, hidden her someplace, left the civic center in a cab—then returned later to get her? It didn't seem likely. After Purrfect had been reported missing, the police and security guards had combed the place and hadn't found her. On the other hand, Winona could have had an accomplice.

One of the waiters approached her. "Ms. Drew?"

"Yes?"

He handed her a piece of paper. "One of the guests asked me to give you this."

"Thank you," Nancy said, taking it from him. It was a note from Gillian:

I have something to give you. It has to do with what we were talking about yesterday. Please meet me at 9:00 on the terrace.

It was five minutes to nine. Nancy glanced around the ballroom, looking for Gillian. But the crowd had grown so thick that it was hard to pick out any faces.

Nancy's eyes settled on the terrace, which was about twenty feet away from where she stood. It was lit with soft outdoor lights, and just beyond it Nancy could see the dark outlines of trees and bushes.

Suddenly Nancy noticed a figure—a man—on the terrace. He was half-hidden behind the edge of the French doors, and he seemed to be watching her.

Her curiosity piqued, Nancy started walking toward him. He looked like Sean!

Just then the man disappeared.

She opened the French doors and walked out to the terrace. The night air was cool, filled with the sweet smells of summer flowers. She looked around, but there was no one there.

On the far edge of the terrace, there were stone steps leading up to a second-floor balcony. An ornate stone railing on the balcony was lined with small pots of red geraniums.

Sean could have run into the garden or gone upstairs, Nancy thought. She decided to try the balcony first.

Nancy headed for the steps, but stopped before she reached them. She'd spotted a small, square object on the ground. It was a few feet to the left of the steps and directly below the railing of the balcony.

Just as she was about to pick it up, however, she heard a scraping sound above her. She looked up quickly—but not quickly enough. A small pot of geraniums crashed down on the side of her head. Nancy cried out in pain before she fell to the ground.

8

Past Crimes

"Ms. Drew."

Nancy heard the voice coming from somewhere far away. She rubbed her eyes and tried to focus. A man's face was hovering over hers. "Ms. Drew, can you hear me?"

His voice sounded familiar. Nancy squinted, trying to see him better. It was Tad.

Nancy tried to sit up, but her head was throbbing too hard. A chill of apprehension went up her spine. Was Tad the person who'd pushed the pot over the balcony railing? Was he here to finish off the job?

"Are you all right, Ms. Drew?" Tad asked.

She could make out his expression now. He looked concerned, not like somebody who was about to do her any harm. "What . . . what happened?" she managed.

"You had a nasty accident," Tad said.

Nancy turned her head slightly. There were pottery shards, dirt, and crushed red geraniums everywhere.

"I came out for a breath of fresh air and saw you lying there," Tad explained. "I went back inside, just long enough to call for the house doctor."

At that moment a middle-aged woman came rushing out to the terrace. She was carrying a black leather bag. She bent down by Nancy's side. "I'm Dr. Donatelli," she said. "I'm glad to see you're conscious. Are you in much pain?"

"Sort of," Nancy said.

Taking some medical instruments out of her bag, Dr. Donatelli began examining her swiftly and efficiently.

"Tad, could you go find Andrea and Bess and George for me?" Nancy asked. "And also a security guard?"

Tad got up. "Sure thing."

After a few minutes the throbbing in Nancy's head had subsided somewhat, and she was able to stand up with Dr. Donatelli's help.

"How does that feel?" the doctor asked her.

Nancy took a tentative step. "Not horrible," she said, grinning weakly.

Two security guards appeared. They took a report from Nancy, assured her that they would try to find out what happened, then headed up to the balcony to investigate.

"You're a very lucky young woman," Dr.

Donatelli told Nancy. "The pot just grazed you on the side of your head. You have a small bump there, and another one on the back of your head, where you hit the ground."

Nancy's eyes lit up. "Oh, good. That means I can go back to the party."

"I'm afraid not," Dr. Donatelli said. "You need to go to the hospital for an X ray."

"You mean now?" Nancy said, grimacing. Her night of investigating was going up in smoke. And where was Gillian?

"I'll take you to the hospital as soon as you feel like walking," Dr. Donatelli said. "I'll call the radiologist right now to set it up."

Just then Bess, George, and Andrea came running out to the terrace. Tad followed close behind.

"Nancy!" Andrea cried. "Are you okay?"

"I'm fine," Nancy reassured her friends.

"I'm going to call the radiologist," Dr. Donatelli told Nancy. "I'll be back shortly."

"Radiologist?" George said, alarmed. "That doesn't sound like you're fine to me."

"I have to get an X ray," Nancy murmured. "I'm sure it's just routine." She explained to her friends what had happened.

"Who could have done this terrible thing to you?" Bess exclaimed.

"I'm not sure," Nancy said. "Tad, did you notice anyone on the balcony when you came out here?"

"No," Tad replied, shaking his head. "I suppose there could have been somebody up there, but I was concentrating on you, so I wasn't really looking."

"What were you doing out here anyway, Nancy?" Bess asked.

At that moment Gillian came through the French doors. "I'm sorry I'm so—" She saw the broken pot of geraniums and Nancy's dirt-covered white dress. "Oh, no. What happened?"

"Just a little accident," Nancy said, smiling.

"A little accident, my foot," Bess said. "Nancy was almost killed by that pot of flowers!"

"Oh, dear," Gillian said anxiously, playing with a lock of her curly brown hair. "If I hadn't been held up . . . if I'd been out here right at nine to meet you, maybe this wouldn't have happened!"

"It's not your fault," Nancy said. "Anyway, I'm okay, so there's nothing to worry about."

"Now that you're in good hands, I guess I'll be getting back to the party," Tad said. "I've got some people I need to talk to."

Nancy thanked him again, and he nodded and left.

"Maybe he's not such a bad guy after all," Bess said in a low voice to Nancy.

Nancy shrugged and turned to Gillian. "I guess we can finish our conversation from yesterday now. But I only have a few minutes."

"Of course." Gillian opened her purse and took out a sealed white envelope. "I wanted to give you this. Inside is a magazine clipping I found last week in Sean's office. He'd be furious if he knew I was giving it to you."

"What is it?" Nancy asked curiously.

"It's . . . well, here, you read it for yourself," Gillian said. "I shouldn't stick around. I don't want Sean to see us together. That's why I was late to begin with."

"What do you mean?" Nancy said.

"I was on my way out here at nine o'clock when I saw him standing just inside the French doors," Gillian explained. "I didn't dare risk having him spot me with you, so I waited until he'd wandered off to the other side of the ballroom."

Nancy considered this news. If the mystery man she had spotted on the terrace had been Sean, that might fit with what Gillian was telling her. Nancy had come out to the terrace a few minutes before nine. Sean could have rushed from his place on the terrace up to the balcony, waited for her, and pushed the pot over the railing. He could have then gone downstairs by some back way and planted himself in the ballroom, just inside the French doors, to watch the outcome. That would explain why Gillian had seen him there at exactly nine o'clock.

"I'd better go now," Gillian said worriedly. "I wouldn't want him to come looking for me."

After Gillian had hurried away, Andrea said, "Does this mean what I think it means? That Sean Dunleavy is a suspect in this case?"

"He might be," Nancy replied, and then filled Andrea in on what Gillian had told her yesterday.

"If that creep lays a finger on my cat—"

"We don't know that he's our thief," Nancy interrupted. "All we have is Gillian's word. Until we get more proof, we can't do anything."

"Speaking of proof, aren't you going to open Gillian's envelope and read the clipping?" George asked Nancy.

"I think it's going to have to wait," Nancy said. "I have to leave for the hospital with Dr. Donatelli, and besides, I want to look for the . . . oh, there it is. Bess, can you pick up that thing on the ground? It's right there, to the left of the steps."

Bess did so and handed the object to Nancy. It was a matchbook.

"The River Inn," Nancy read. "Hmm."

"What's so interesting about a matchbook from the River Inn?" George asked.

"I was reaching down to pick it up when I got hit on the head," Nancy replied. "It could have been planted there by my assailant, to lure me to that spot." She paused. "I also saw a man out here, just before I arrived. This matchbook could have belonged to him."

"Do you think *he* could have pushed the pot?" Andrea asked nervously.

"I don't know." Nancy put the envelope and the matchbook into her purse. "Listen, while I'm at the hospital, can you girls do some sleuthing for me here, then meet me at my house?"

"What kind of sleuthing?" George asked.

"Go up to the balcony and find out where it

77

leads to," Nancy said. "Then make a round of our suspects and see where they all were at nine o'clock. Talk to Winona, Sean, Tad, Kara—"

"Kara!" Andrea cried out. "You suspect her, too? But why?"

"George and Bess will explain it to you," Nancy said. "Don't worry, Andrea, we're just trying to cover all the bases."

Nancy didn't get home from the hospital until eleven o'clock. George, Bess, and Andrea were waiting for her in the living room, along with Carson and Hannah.

"Oh, Nancy!" Hannah cried, hugging the girl as she came through the front door. "You should have called us. Are you all right?"

"I'm fine," Nancy said, hugging her back. "The X ray confirmed it. All I have is a big fat headache and a couple of little bumps."

"Your friends told us what happened," Carson said worriedly. "I'm just glad your injuries weren't more serious."

After being reassured that Nancy was all right, Carson went to his study to finish going over some papers, and Hannah went to bed.

"Are you really okay?" Andrea asked Nancy.

"I really am," Nancy said, plopping down on the couch. "But I'm anxious to look at Gillian's clipping. I didn't have a minute to myself at the hospital."

She pulled the envelope out of her purse and

ripped it open. George sat down next to her and peeked at it over her shoulder.

"Wow, guys, listen to this headline!" George exclaimed. "'Dunleavy Accused of Foul Play at Liverpool Cat Show'!"

"What?" Andrea said.

Nancy scanned the article quickly. "The article goes on to say that Sean Dunleavy allegedly slipped a mild tranquilizer into the food of a rival breeder's prize Siamese cat," she explained. "At the time the article was written, an investigation was under way to see whether the charges could be proved."

"Well, what do you know?" Bess remarked. "I guess our guy isn't above messing with the competition after all."

"What I want to know is, what became of the investigation? This article is dated last October," Nancy said. "After all, this information wouldn't be too useful to us if it turned out Sean had been wrongfully accused."

"Still, you have to admit that it's a weird coincidence," Andrea said.

"That's true," Nancy replied thoughtfully. "I think I'll follow this up with Gillian first thing tomorrow."

"Good idea," Bess said.

Nancy put the clipping back in her purse. "So, tell me what you three ace detectives found at the country club. Any juicy clues?"

"Well, we tried to trace your attacker's exit

route," George said. "The balcony is at the end of a long hallway on the second floor. And off the hallway there are three stairways that lead back down to the ballroom."

"Did you see anyone upstairs?" Nancy asked.

"Nope. It was absolutely deserted," George replied. "Anyway, we timed it, and your attacker could have pushed the pot of geraniums, run into the hallway, and gone back down to the party in a matter of seconds."

"Did you guys get a chance to talk to our suspects?" Nancy asked.

"We sure did," Andrea said. "I spoke to Winona Bell. She claimed she was at the buffet table at nine, getting food. One of the men working there confirmed it."

"I tackled Sean Dunleavy," Bess said with a groan. "He said he was wandering around looking for Gillian at nine. When I asked him if he'd been on the terrace at any time, he said, 'Why don't you go find some poor chap to dance with instead of torturing me with your childish games?' and left in a huff. Can you imagine?"

"That's Sean Dunleavy for you," Nancy said.

"I covered Kara and Tad," George said. "Kara said she was talking to a group of people near the buffet, but she couldn't remember who, and I couldn't get anyone to back her up on that."

"Did you ask Neal?" Nancy said.

"Yup," George replied. "He said he lost track of Kara from quarter to nine to nine-fifteen or so.

He was busy chatting up one of Simon-Ross's clients."

Nancy nodded. "And Tad?"

"He said he was heading out to the terrace for fresh air, like he told you," George said. "And just before that, he was having a long conversation with a fellow board member from the cat shelter, a Mrs. Gross. I talked to her, and she backed up his story."

Nancy touched her head gingerly. "Before I do any more work on this case, I think I need a good night's sleep," she said. "I'm sure you all do, too."

As they stood up to go, Andrea said, "I don't like how this is all turning out, Nancy. If Sean Dunleavy, or whoever, is trying to hurt you because of Purrfect—"

"I promise you I'll be very careful," Nancy said.

"You'd better be, Nan," Bess said worriedly. "What happened tonight was serious stuff."

Early the next day Nancy called the River Inn.

"Good morning," she said cheerfully. "I happened to be down the block from your inn last night, and I found a bag of cat grooming tools—very expensive ones, from what I can tell. Anyway, it just occurred to me that, with the big cat show in town, these might belong to one of your guests."

"Of course," the desk clerk said. "We have a

few guests here who are attending the cat show."
There was a long pause. Nancy could hear him
punching up a file on a computer.

"Here we go," he said. "Mr. Dunleavy, room
forty-five, and Ms. Samms, room forty-six. Would
you like me to leave a message for them and have
them call you?"

"Actually, I'm going to be in your neighborhood later on, so I'll just drop by with the bag and
ask them myself," Nancy replied. "Thank you for
your help."

Nancy headed for the River Inn right after
breakfast. Her head felt much better, although
she still had a trace of a headache.

She planned to try to see Gillian alone, before
the young woman left for the civic center, to find
out if she or Sean carried matches. She also
wanted to ask Gillian about the Liverpool Cat
Show investigation, to see if anything had been
proved about Sean's guilt or innocence.

Nancy parked her Mustang in front of the River
Inn and walked briskly into the lobby. Suddenly
she spotted Sean getting out of an elevator.
Thinking quickly, she stepped behind a marble
column.

The Englishman never noticed her. Scanning
a newspaper headline, Dunleavy wandered
through the lobby and out the revolving door.

Sighing with relief, Nancy made her way to the
elevator and pushed the button for the fourth
floor. Once there, she looked down the hallway
and saw that a few of the doors were open. The

maid must be cleaning the rooms, Nancy thought.

Nancy went by Gillian's room. The door was open, but the young woman wasn't there. Sean's door, across the hall, was also open.

Quickly Nancy walked into Sean's room. It was spacious and elegantly decorated, with a view of downtown River Heights. She glanced around, then slipped into the closet. After a moment the maid came in with some fresh towels, then left, locking the door after her.

Her heart racing, Nancy stepped out of the closet and began searching Sean's room.

On the nightstand was a carafe of water, a box of tissues, and a "Welcome to River Heights" brochure. The dresser drawers contained only clothing.

Just then Nancy heard a key in the door. She froze in apprehension. In a matter of seconds she would be caught red-handed!

9

Close Call

Nancy rushed to the closet and managed to get the door half-closed before the person walked into the room.

She stood very still, buried in suits and jackets, barely breathing. Her back was pressed painfully against a wall hook, but she was afraid to move on the chance that she might be heard.

"Now, where is that umbrella?" the person muttered. It was Sean.

Nancy heard his footsteps growing nearer. He was coming toward the closet! Nancy stiffened with fear.

Just then the phone began to ring. Sean grunted, then went to answer it.

"Yes? Gillian, where are you?" he asked gruffly. "At the gym down the street? Well, get back here and get changed. No, you can't stick around for the aerobics class. We've got a lot of work to do. I'm on my way to the civic center now. Meet me there as soon as you can."

He hung up and started for the closet again. Nancy held her breath. Just then Nancy heard him say, "Ah, here it is."

A moment later he was out of the room. That was a little too close for comfort, she thought.

Nancy waited for a few minutes, just to be safe, then continued to search the room. She turned the light on in the closet and looked for Purrfect's cage or any sign that the Persian had been hidden there. She found a round-trip plane ticket and a passport on top of the dresser, along with some magazines and a map of Chicago. Then she checked in the bathroom and under the bed. "Nothing," she said with a sigh as she went to the door. Poking her head out, she looked up and down the hallway, to see if anyone had spotted her. No one was there.

When Nancy got off the elevator in the lobby, Gillian was just coming in. The young woman was wearing a tan jogging suit and tennis shoes, and her face was damp with perspiration.

"Nancy, what are you doing here?" Gillian whispered, glancing around nervously.

"I was looking for you," Nancy replied. "It's okay, Sean's left." She put her hand on Gillian's elbow and led her to a sitting area. Once they were seated, Nancy said, "Do you carry matches?"

Gillian's eyes widened in surprise. "That's a funny question. The answer is no."

"How about Sean?" Nancy asked.

Gillian frowned. "I suppose he might. I've seen him smoking a pipe from time to time."

"Just one more thing," Nancy continued. "About that clipping you gave me. What ever came of that charge? Was Sean found guilty of tampering with the cat food?"

Gillian shrugged apologetically. "I'm sorry, I actually don't know. I just came across that article last week, and I haven't had time to look into it. You see, I only started working for Sean a few months ago, so I don't know much about his history."

"I understand," Nancy said.

"Still, it's very suspicious, don't you think?" Gillian remarked, smoothing back a lock of her curly brown hair. "I mean, doesn't there seem to be some sort of connection between the Liverpool incident and Purrfect's kidnapping?"

"I'm not sure yet. But thanks for the lead. I'll look into it and see what I can find out." With that Nancy said goodbye and left the River Inn.

When Nancy got home, Hannah told her that Bess had called. Nancy phoned her back right away.

"Hi, Nan," Bess said. "How are you feeling?"

"Much better," Nancy said, propping her feet up on a chair.

"I'm glad to hear that," Bess replied. "Guess what? I've made some progress on the case!"

Nancy sat up quickly. "Great, I could use some good news. What's up?"

"I've got a lunch date with Neal!" Bess announced exuberantly.

Nancy laughed.

"What's so funny?" Bess asked. "I mean, so it's a lunch date. I still plan to pump him for information about his boss."

"You're right, Bess," Nancy said seriously. "This case is getting so bogged down, we need some fresh facts. Get everything you can on Kara—without arousing Neal's suspicions, of course."

"Of course," Bess said. "I'll call you later. Neal's meeting me at one o'clock."

"Where are you going?" Nancy asked.

"Juanita's. They have yummy guacamole dip and chicken fajitas."

"Well, have fun," Nancy told her.

After hanging up, Nancy leaned back against her chair, deep in thought. She got the magazine clipping that Gillian had given her out of her bag and read it again. Then she picked up the phone and dialed George's number.

"George? Are you free for lunch? Terrific, come on over. I'll make some club sandwiches. But first, I'd like to ask you to do a little errand for me."

* * *

George walked into the Drews' house carrying a huge pile of magazines. Her purple windbreaker was dripping wet, and her short, dark hair clung to her forehead.

"A trip to the library in the rain," she grumbled good-naturedly. "Those club sandwiches had better be good."

Nancy relieved George of the magazines. "You're a trooper. Thanks so much for doing this."

George took off her windbreaker and ran a hand through her hair. "I got all the back issues of every cat magazine the library had—*Cat Crazy, Famous Felines,* and *Paw Prints.* What are we going to do with them, anyway?"

Nancy filled her friend in on her talk with Gillian. "So, since Gillian doesn't know what ever came of the charges against Sean, I thought we might do a little research in these magazines. From what Andrea tells me, they cover the international cat scene pretty thoroughly."

"Sounds like a good plan," George said, nodding.

The girls settled on the living room floor and began their work. Nancy turned on the radio so they'd have some soothing music in the background.

Hannah brought in the plate of sandwiches Nancy had made, two cans of soda, and a bowl of potato chips.

"It's so nice to see the two of you relaxing over

some magazines instead of chasing criminals," the housekeeper said merrily.

George and Nancy exchanged an amused glance.

"Well, actually, Hannah, we *are* chasing criminals," Nancy confessed. "We're trying to find a cat thief." She told the older woman about the case.

"That poor cat," Hannah murmured sympathetically. "I hope her abductor is taking good care of her, at least."

"I'm sure Purrfect is okay," Nancy reassured her. If only I could feel certain of that, Nancy thought.

The girls ate the delicious sandwiches and continued leafing through the magazines.

"There sure are a lot of cute cats," George remarked after a while. "Look at this little gray kitten. Makes me want to get one of my own."

"I know it," Nancy agreed. She lingered over a photo spread of Persians and thought of Purrfect. George sat up suddenly. "Hey!"

"What?"

She held up the copy of *Cat Crazy* she'd been reading. "Here it is, Nancy. A whole story on Sean Dunleavy and the Liverpool Cat Show scandal!"

10

Double Disaster

"Great!" Nancy said eagerly. "Now maybe we can get some answers."

George began reading the article out loud. " 'Sean Dunleavy—undisputed king of the British cat scene—faced his biggest obstacle yet at the Liverpool Cat Show in October. Rival exhibitor Anthony Kruger charged that Dunleavy slipped a mild tranquilizer into the food of Kruger's prize Siamese, Orpheus. Kruger claimed that Dunleavy, whose star entrant in the show was a young Siamese named Stockings, was trying to improve his cat's chances of winning. Dunleavy angrily denied the accusations and demanded an investigation.

" 'The Liverpool Cat Show board has just concluded its investigation, and it has found no proof to support Kruger's charges. So Sean Dunleavy is vindicated. And for those of you who are interested, Orpheus is in fine shape. Kruger plans to enter him in the upcoming London show.'"

George threw up her hands. "Oh, well, so much for that lead."

"It doesn't mean Sean isn't guilty of stealing Purrfect, though," Nancy reminded her. "We still have to consider Gillian's suspicions. Plus the fact that Sean may or may not have been on the country club terrace right before that pot of geraniums fell on my head."

"That's true," George said.

Nancy frowned. "But on the other hand, can we trust Gillian's word that Sean was nowhere to be found around the time Purrfect was stolen? What if she's setting him up?"

"He does treat her pretty rotten," George commented.

"Besides, I'm not a hundred percent positive the man on the terrace was Sean," Nancy continued. "Even though he may have dropped that matchbook from the River Inn."

"This is getting complicated," George remarked, reaching for a potato chip.

Nancy lay down on the floor and stared thoughtfully at the ceiling. "And I sure didn't find anything suspicious when I checked his room this morning."

George's eyes widened. "You sneaked into his room? Nancy, are you crazy? He could have caught you."

"Just doing my job, ma'am," Nancy said with a grin. "Anyway, Sean didn't catch me."

Just then the doorbell rang. "I'll get it, Hannah!" Nancy called out, getting up.

It was Bess.

"Hi, guys!" she said, slipping off her raincoat. Underneath, she was wearing a short yellow skirt and a flowered top. "Isn't it a gorgeous day?"

George frowned. "Am I hearing things? It's pouring out there."

"She had a lunch date," Nancy explained. "With Neal."

George smiled knowingly. "Uh-huh. And was this a *business* lunch?"

Bess blushed. "For your information, Ms. Fayne, it was. Sort of. What I mean is—"

"I asked her to find out everything she could about Kara Kramer," Nancy told George.

"And I did. Wait till you hear!" Bess glanced at the plate of sandwiches on the coffee table. "Hey, what's that?"

"Our lunch," George said. "So? What did you find out?"

Bess plopped down on the floor. "Well," she began, helping herself to a sandwich, "it turns out that our Ms. Kramer is a very devious woman."

"Devious? What do you mean?" Nancy asked.

"According to Neal, Kara just joined Simon-Ross Media about a year ago. Before that she was with some big firm in New York City. Neal says

that Kara's got kind of a bad rep in the industry."
Bess leaned forward eagerly. "Apparently, she
has a history of pulling really sneaky publicity
stunts to help out her campaigns."

Nancy's curiosity was aroused. "What sorts of
stunts?"

"Well, once Kara was doing a new campaign for
Citrus Sunshine orange juice," Bess explained.
"She somehow managed to spread a rumor that
the spokeswoman for their competitor, Tangy
Tropics, was actually allergic to oranges and had
never tasted Tangy Tropics in her life. This wasn't
true, but the rumor really hurt Tangy Tropics for
a while and boosted Citrus Sunshine sales. Of
course, no one ever managed to prove Kara
started the rumor, but a lot of people knew it was
her, just the same."

"Hmm," George said, glancing at Nancy, who
was about to speak.

"Wait, there's more," Bess said. "Neal says that
the Kitty Classics campaign is crucial to Kara's
career. She's on the brink of a huge promotion,
and this campaign will be the deciding factor."

"So what do you say, Nan?" George asked. "Do
you think Kara kidnapped Purrfect as another
one of her publicity stunts?"

"It seems possible," Nancy replied slowly. "If
Neal is telling the truth, that is."

"Of course he's telling the truth!" Bess protested. "Why wouldn't he?"

Nancy smiled apologetically. "I'm sorry, Bess.

It's just my suspicious nature. Anyway, I'm sure you're right. Kara's memo to her boss seems to fit in with Neal's account."

"So," George said, "we have on our hands one publicity hound and one missing Persian. What does that add up to?"

Nancy glanced at her watch. "I'd like to stop by Kara's office, but it's too late today. Maybe tomorrow. If I could just catch Kara off guard, she might tell me something she doesn't want me to know."

The next morning Nancy got ready to pay another call on Kara Kramer. She had a quick breakfast of cereal, orange juice, and toast and dressed in jeans, a white T-shirt, and sneakers.

Before she left, Nancy called Bess. Her friend answered after several rings.

After saying hello Nancy told Bess, "I was thinking that whoever stole Purrfect might have taken her to a kennel for safekeeping. So it might be a good idea if we checked the kennels in the area, just to cover all the bases. Do you think you and George could do that?"

"Sure," Bess replied. "But what about you?"

"Well, right now I'm on my way to see Kara. And after that I'm going to stop in at the civic center to snoop around Sean's booth."

"What are you trying to find?" Bess asked.

"I'm not sure. But my instincts keep telling me to zero in on Sean and Kara."

"So, tell me what George and I are supposed to do with this kennel thing," Bess said.

"Well, if Purrfect is in a kennel at all, she'll be hidden away," Nancy said. "So maybe while one of you is being given a tour, the other could wander around the place getting lost, if you know what I mean."

"I know what you mean," Bess said. "For example, I could distract the person who's giving us the tour, while George goes off and pokes around."

"Right," Nancy said. "And if you guys happen to find Purrfect, come get me. I'll either be at Simon-Ross, the civic center, or home."

"Okay," Bess agreed.

After saying goodbye, Nancy headed for Simon-Ross Media.

The Simon-Ross receptionist was busy talking on the phone when Nancy approached the desk.

After waiting patiently for a moment Nancy cleared her throat.

The receptionist looked up at her.

"Yes, miss? Can I help you?"

"I'd like to see Kara Kramer, please," Nancy told her with a smile.

"Do you have an appointment?"

"No, but if you'll just tell her it's Nancy Drew and that I need to see—" Nancy began.

The receptionist punched a button on the phone console. "Neal, there's a Nancy Drew here to see Ms. Kramer. What? Okay, I'll tell her."

"Ms. Kramer isn't here, but her assistant will speak to you," the receptionist announced. "He'll be right out."

The receptionist returned to her conversation, and Nancy waited for Neal.

He appeared shortly. "Sorry to keep you waiting," he said, smiling apologetically. "Come on in."

Neal led her to a small cubicle outside Kara's office. When they were seated, he said, "Kara's not here right now. Is there something I could help you with?"

"Actually, I need to speak to her personally. It's about something she told me the other day about the Kitty Classics campaign," Nancy explained vaguely. "Do you know when she'll be back?"

Neal ran a hand through his wavy auburn hair. "She left here about half an hour ago. Didn't say where she was going or when she'd return."

Nancy frowned. Suddenly she noticed a framed poster over Neal's desk. It was an advertisement for the River Inn!

"Nice poster," she remarked casually. "Is the River Inn a client of Simon-Ross Media?"

"Yup," Neal replied. "Kara got that account about six months ago."

Nancy rose. "Well, sorry to trouble you. Please tell Kara I came by."

"Say hi to Bess for me," Neal said.

As Nancy walked to her car, her mind was racing. Could the River Inn matchbook have belonged to Kara? Had she pushed the pot of geraniums over the balcony? She and Sean were the only ones without a solid alibi for the time of the incident.

Nancy looked at her watch and saw that it was almost noon. She decided to head to the civic center right away.

When Nancy walked into the civic center auditorium at a quarter to one, a great commotion greeted her.

Something was terribly wrong. There were security guards and policemen running around. Noticing that a big crowd had gathered around one of the galleries, Nancy headed briskly in that direction. When she got there, she found Sean lying on the ground in the backstage area, moaning in pain. A doctor was tending to a huge bump on the back of his head. A dozen or so bystanders were milling about.

Sean looked up and spotted Nancy. "You didn't work fast enough," he said dryly.

"What do you mean?" Nancy asked, alarmed. "What happened to you?"

"The cat thief came back," Sean muttered. "I was knocked out. And Desdemona is gone!"

11

The Mystery Woman

Desdemona had been stolen!

Nancy couldn't believe it. She knelt down by Sean's side. "Can you tell me about it?" She turned to the doctor who was attending him. "That is, if it's okay for him to talk?"

"Keep it brief," the doctor instructed. "Mr. Dunleavy's head injury is minor, but he needs to get to the hospital to get it checked out, then back to his hotel room for some rest."

"Of course," Nancy replied.

A police officer entered the backstage area just then and addressed the crowd of people around Sean. "If you could all gather over here, I need to ask some questions."

The crowd followed the police officer to a corner of the room. Nancy was left alone with Sean and the doctor.

"I already told this story to the police and the security guards," Sean said to Nancy. "But I'll tell it again. I'd brought Desdemona back here to get her ready for a one o'clock showing of Persians. The next thing I knew, I felt a blow on the back of my head. When I came to, Desdemona was gone."

"Did you see or hear anything just before you were attacked?" Nancy asked. "Anything that might help identify the thief? Think carefully—it's very important."

Sean frowned. "No, nothing."

"Was Desdemona in a portable carrier, or had you taken her out of it?" Nancy queried.

"I'd taken her out of it," Sean answered.

Nancy nodded. "Was anyone else back here?"

"No, no one. The place was deserted. Actually, I was rather surprised that—"

Just then Gillian came running in carrying a small bottle. "Why are all these people—" She stopped short when she saw Sean. "Oh, no! What happened?"

Nancy explained the situation. "Sean's going to be okay, though."

Gillian turned white. "But the thief has Desdemona?"

Nancy nodded.

"Oh, dear!" The young woman's eyes filled with tears. "If only I'd stayed by Sean's side, this wouldn't have happened."

"Isn't it funny how you're never around when I need you, Gillian?" Sean said snidely.

Nancy glanced at the bottle in Gillian's hand. "Were you running an errand, or something?"

"I'd forgotten the grooming powder in my car. I had to go out and get it before the showing," Gillian told her.

"We'd better be going, Mr. Dunleavy," the doctor spoke up. He helped Sean to his feet. The Englishman stood up groggily. Gillian rushed to his side and took his arm.

"Gillian, the doctor is taking me to the hospital," Sean mumbled. "You stay here. I want you to keep an eye on the other cats. Go!"

"All right," Gillian replied in a trembling voice as she headed for the main hall.

Sean and the doctor left. The policeman had finished questioning the crowd, and the backstage area was nearly empty. However, a middle-aged man and a woman lingered, talking.

Nancy sauntered over to them. "Isn't this terrible?" she said casually. "Two cat thefts in one week!"

The man nodded. "It's a disgrace. I was just saying to the police officer, the security staff here isn't doing its job."

"Maybe they'll find the thief now, with the information you gave them," the woman spoke up, smiling at him.

"Oh? What information?" Nancy asked.

"I was just telling the police officer, I noticed something out in the parking lot about fifteen minutes ago," the man said.

Nancy's eyes lit up. "Really?"

100

The man shrugged. "It might be nothing, I don't know. But when I was walking through the lot on my way into the building, I noticed a woman running from one of the back exits. She was carrying something."

"What was it?" Nancy asked eagerly.

"A bundle, or a bag, or some other bulky-looking thing. I'm not sure," the man replied.

"Can you describe her?" Nancy prompted.

"She had dark hair," the man said. "That's about all I can tell you. I didn't think much about it at the time."

Nancy nodded. "Which back exit was it, can you remember?"

The man squinted thoughtfully. "When you're facing the building from the parking lot, it's two doors from the right."

"I'm sure the police were glad to get this information," Nancy told him.

"Suppose so," the man said as he turned to go. "Come on, Mabel. Let's go get a cup of coffee."

Left alone, Nancy suddenly realized that she was in the backstage area of gallery three—the same area where Purrfect had been stolen. Her eyes went straight to the blue door. Had Sean's assailant taken this route to the parking lot?

She went quickly to the blue door and opened it. The stairwell on the other side was still dark and musty-smelling. The cat thief and I may be the only ones who use this exit, she thought wryly.

Taking her flashlight out of her purse, Nancy

made her way slowly down the stairs. When she got to the bottom, she opened the door leading out to the parking lot. She stepped outside and turned around. The exit she'd just come out of was two doors from the right!

So maybe the dark-haired woman is our thief after all, Nancy mused.

Just then a police officer came up to her. He peered suspiciously at the flashlight in her hand. "Excuse me, miss, can I help you?"

He probably thinks I'm the cat thief, Nancy thought with amusement. She proceeded to explain who she was and what she was doing. "So naturally, I'm curious about Desdemona's disappearance, since it seems linked to Purrfect's."

The police officer nodded. "This thief is a slippery one. We're following up a lead right now and searching for a dark-haired woman who was seen leaving this exit with a package. But so far, nothing's turned up."

Nancy looked out at the parking lot and saw two officers going up and down the aisles.

"Well, good luck," Nancy said to the police officer. "I'll go upstairs and see if I can turn up anything there."

She went back inside the door and, as she started up the stairs, something caught her eye. "Hey, what's this?" she said out loud.

On the fourth step the beam of her flashlight had fallen on a sparkling object. Nancy bent down to pick it up. It was a large, clear, oval-shaped rhinestone with some dried-up glue on the back of it. She studied it for a second. Nancy recalled that Desdemona, like Purrfect, wore a rhinestone collar.

She put it in her pocket, intending to head to Sean's booth to ask Gillian whether Desdemona had been wearing her rhinestone collar when she was stolen.

But the young woman wasn't at her booth. Nancy waited for a few minutes, then gave up.

"I guess Sean's right," Nancy said to herself. "Gillian *does* take long breaks."

Nancy headed for the phone booths. She wanted to get in touch with Bess and Kara.

Walking through the crowded aisles, Nancy thought about the unexpected turn the case had taken. Sean was no longer a suspect. And the thief, whoever it was, had not been interested in just Purrfect.

At the phone booth Nancy dialed Bess's number.

"Poor Desdemona!" Bess exclaimed when Nancy told her the news. "This case is getting crazier by the minute."

"I know it," Nancy said. "Did you and George have any luck with the kennels?"

"'Fraid not," Bess answered. "We've tried three so far, and no silver Persians. We're going to try two more after lunch, though."

"Great."

When Nancy called Simon-Ross Media, she

was told that Kara had some business appointments and was not coming back to the office until the next day.

"Do you want to leave a message?" the receptionist asked her.

"No, no message."

As Nancy hung up, an idea suddenly came to her.

Kara liked flashy costume jewelry. Could the large rhinestone have fallen off one of her earrings or bracelets—not Desdemona's collar?

Kara also had dark hair. And she hadn't been in her office during the time of Desdemona's abduction.

Had Kara Kramer gone as far as to steal a second cat in order to divert suspicion from Purrfect's disappearance?

12

The Stars of Tanzania

Nancy quickly decided on a plan of action. She would check up on Sean Dunleavy to see if he had any more information. He might have seen Kara hanging around his booth in the last few days. He might also remember something about Desdemona's abduction that would tie the crime to Kara. Plus, Nancy wanted to show him the rhinestone she'd found.

She headed for the River Inn, hoping that Sean would be back from the hospital. She found him in his room, reading a magazine in bed.

"How are you feeling?" Nancy asked him.

"I tried to sleep, but I couldn't," he told her. "The police came by just a few minutes ago. Bumbling bunch. And now my head is throbbing."

"I'm sorry," she said. "Can I get you anything? Some aspirin? Tea?"

"Nothing, thanks," Sean replied. "Just catch whoever did this to me and get Desdemona back."

"That's exactly what I'd like to do," Nancy declared.

"This cat thief is clever, whoever it is," Sean continued. "After all the precautions I took, he still managed to find me alone, knock me out, and make off with my prize Persian."

"You took precautions?" Nancy said.

"After that other Persian disappeared—what was its name, Puffy?"

"Purrfect," Nancy corrected.

Sean nodded. "Purrfect, right. Anyway, after she disappeared, I figured there might be a cat thief, maybe a Persian thief, on the loose. So I made sure that either Gillian or I would be manning the booth at all times. And at night I took the trouble of boarding my cats at a kennel. A place called Le Pet Spa."

"Do you know Kara Kramer?" Nancy asked him.

Sean looked thoughtful. "No, I can't say that I do."

"She's an advertising executive at a local agency called Simon-Ross Media," Nancy told him. "Tall, slender, about forty or forty-five. Black hair cut in a pageboy. Maybe you've seen her around your booth."

Sean shrugged. "I don't think so, but I'm not sure."

The phone rang just then.

"Who's decided to bother me now?" Sean muttered, picking it up. "Yes? What? No, I do *not* want a side of potato salad to go with my roast beef sandwich, because I did not order a roast beef sandwich to begin with!"

He slammed down the phone. "After the day I've had, this is all I need. Or I should say, after the week I've had. I tell you, Ms. Drew, this has been a nightmare of a trip."

"What do you mean?" Nancy asked him curiously.

"What do I mean? Where do I begin?" Sean laughed bitterly. "To begin with, there was our flight. We were detained at the airport in London for not one, not two, but *three hours* by customs officials. They searched everybody's baggage because of some sort of police action."

"What sort of police action?" Nancy inquired.

Sean shrugged. "Some big robbery the night before. I guess the customs officials were hoping to nab the thieves on their way out of the country." Sean paused and reached for a glass of water from his nightstand. He took a sip. "The point is, we were extremely rushed once we got to the cat show, which was not pleasant, believe me."

"I'm sure," Nancy murmured sympathetically. An image flashed in her mind of Sean on the first day of the show, complaining loudly to Gillian about how late they were. Sean had also mentioned something about flight delays to Nancy when she first met him.

"And then, right away, that Persian gets stolen, which of course made me afraid for my own cats," Sean went on.

"Are your other cats Persians, too?" Nancy asked. So far, the thief only seemed to be interested in Persians.

"No, just Desdemona," Sean answered. "And now"—he threw his hands up in the air dramatically—"this happens. I'm bedridden, and the best show cat I've ever had is in the hands of some fiend."

"I'll do my best to get Desdemona back—her and Purrfect," Nancy promised. "One last thing," she said, pulling the rhinestone out of her pocket. "Do you recognize this?"

"It looks like a stone from a cat collar," Sean replied after a moment. "Some collars are studded all the way around with these things. Look in that bag on my dresser. I think I've got one in there."

Nancy found a white leather collar in the bag. There were ten rhinestones mounted on it altogether—rhinestones that looked nearly identical to the one Nancy had found.

"Was Desdemona wearing this kind of collar when she was stolen?" Nancy asked Sean.

Sean nodded. "All my cats do. It's a fairly common cat collar."

Nancy remembered just then that she'd seen a similar collar on Purrfect.

"I found this on the stairs off the backstage area of gallery three," Nancy told Sean, showing him the rhinestone. "Do you think it could have fallen off Desdemona's collar while the thief was carrying her to the parking lot?"

"That's probably what happened," Sean said. "These collars are cheaply made. I'm sure it doesn't take much to knock one of these rhinestones loose."

Seeing that Sean was tired, Nancy stood up to go. "Why don't you get some rest?" she suggested. "I'll check back with you later."

"All right," Sean muttered. "I'd better take my phone off the hook for a while, though. I don't want to be woken up by a call about potato salad, or roast beef, or similar nonsense."

As Nancy walked to the elevator, she thought about the rhinestone. Whether it was from Desdemona's collar or Kara Kramer's jewelry, Nancy was still in the same boat. The blue door in the backstage area of gallery three was probably the thief's escape route. The dark-haired mystery woman was probably the thief.

Kara had to be the culprit, Nancy said to herself. The only other dark-haired woman in the case was Gillian.

Nancy frowned. Gillian *had* been at the cat show both times when the thefts had taken place. And she'd been at the country club when the flowerpot incident had occurred. But why would she have stolen the cats? Nancy figured that Gillian might have taken Purrfect, then tried to pin the crime on Sean. It might have been some sort of retaliation for his rotten treatment of her. But what reason could Gillian have had to knock Sean on the head and abduct Desdemona, especially when she'd had constant access to the cat? It didn't make sense.

Nancy checked her watch. Four o'clock. She made a quick call to Bess's house and learned from Mrs. Marvin that both Bess and George were at the Faynes'. Nancy decided to drop by and see if they'd made any progress with the kennels.

"You're just in time for tea and cookies," Bess said cheerfully when Nancy walked in the door. "Fresh from the oven. Chocolate chip with macadamia nuts."

Nancy chuckled. "Sounds great. It's been a long day."

"You're telling me," George moaned. She was lying on the couch. "We must have visited every kennel in town."

"Any luck?" Nancy asked.

Bess handed Nancy a mug of tea. "Nope. We ran into some Persians, but no silver ones."

"How about you, Nan?" George inquired. "Have you made any progress?"

Nancy filled her two friends in on the afternoon's events.

"Have you got any new leads?" George asked.

"A few. I have a clue to pursue, anyway." Nancy pulled the rhinestone out of her pocket.

"Nancy!" Bess cried out. "You found a *diamond!*"

Nancy grinned. "I wish. This is just a rhinestone. It probably fell off Desdemona's collar while the thief was abducting her, although I was also thinking that it might be from Kara Kramer's—"

Nancy stopped just then. Her blue eyes widened.

"Nan? What is it?" George said.

Nancy stood up. "Come on. We have an errand to run."

"Where're we going?" Bess queried.

Nancy was already halfway out the door. "We've got to get to the library right away. I think I just figured out a very important part of our puzzle."

George and Bess went in search of a table while Nancy spoke to the librarian.

"I'd like to see the London *Times*. The last week's issues, please, if you have them."

The librarian disappeared, then returned with a large pile. He handed them to her. "There you go, miss."

Nancy thanked him and went to find her friends. They were sitting alone in the deserted reading room.

Nancy dropped the newspapers on the table.

"The London *Times*," George noted. "What are you up to now?"

"A hunch," Nancy replied mysteriously. "Start going through these for anything on a robbery, okay?"

"What kind of robbery?" Bess asked.

"Anything that has to do with jewelry. Maybe diamonds. And I believe it took place last Sunday," Nancy replied.

"Here's something," George said after a few minutes. She handed a page to Nancy. "A heist involving some big jewelry store."

Nancy scanned the article quickly. "Last Sunday night Tate's Jewelers in London was robbed," Nancy said. "The thieves made off with a set of very famous diamonds called the Stars of Tanzania."

There was a photograph of the diamonds. They were large and oval-shaped. And there were ten of them.

Nancy pulled out the rhinestone from her pocket and looked at it thoughtfully. Then she exclaimed, "It looks like a perfect match to the Stars of Tanzania!"

"The suspense is killing me!" Bess burst out. "Tell us, Nan—what does this robbery have to do with anything?"

"Your comment about this rhinestone looking like a diamond gave me the idea, Bess," Nancy replied. "Plus Sean's story about the holdup in customs on Monday morning. See this?" She lined up the rhinestone with one of the diamonds in the photograph. They were shown actual size in the picture.

"They're the same size and shape," George remarked.

Bess leaned forward with a puzzled expression on her face. "So how do you think these diamonds are connected to Purrfect and Desdemona?"

"I haven't quite figured out the details yet, but I have a theory," Nancy explained. "What if the English diamond thieves, whoever they were, used Desdemona's collar to smuggle the Stars of Tanzania out of London? They could have taken the rhinestones off Desdemona's collar and mounted the diamonds in their place. The collar Sean showed me had ten rhinestones. There are ten of these Stars of Tanzania. Then, once Desdemona was safely through London customs and in the United States, someone would have retrieved the collar—maybe an American contact."

George whistled. "That's some theory."

"Are you saying that Sean and Gillian are part of a smuggling ring, then?" Bess asked incredulously.

"I'm not sure," Nancy replied. "Especially considering that Sean was attacked by someone. That bump on his head is pretty real. He and Gillian could have been used as unwitting pawns in the whole scheme, though, and not have known they were smuggling diamonds. Or"— Nancy paused, frowning—"Gillian could be the guilty one."

"Gillian!" Bess exclaimed. "How could she be a smuggler? She's so sweet and shy."

"Hmm," Nancy said. "But it makes sense. She has dark hair. She could have dropped the River Inn matchbook to set me up at the country club. And she was at the show both times when the cat thefts took place."

"But why would Gillian, or whoever the thief is, need to steal Desdemona? Why not steal just the collar?" George asked.

"I don't know," Nancy replied after a moment. "Maybe the thief wanted to make absolute sure that no one would tie the London diamond heist to Desdemona's collar."

"So stealing all of Desdemona, and not just her collar, could have been a smokescreen," George said.

Nancy nodded. "Right. And stealing Purrfect set the whole thing up. It gave everyone the illusion that there was a cat thief, or a Persian thief, on the loose."

Bess looked troubled. "If Gillian is the one, though, why would she need to conk Sean on the head? She had access to Desdemona all the time. She could have just taken her."

"That bothers me, too," Nancy said. "But you know, after Purrfect disappeared, Sean really got obsessive about protecting Desdemona. Maybe Gillian couldn't get her alone long enough to steal her and finally got desperate enough to resort to violence."

114

"I suppose," Bess murmured.

"I know this all sounds pretty wild," Nancy admitted. "But it's hard to ignore the fact that there are ten large, oval-shaped rhinestones on Desdemona's collar, and ten large, oval-shaped diamonds missing from Tate's Jewelers. They *must* be connected."

Nancy returned to the London *Times* article on the robbery. "It says here that the heist took place on Sunday, probably between six and eight P.M. Sean's flight left London on Monday morning. That means that the thieves would have had to mount the diamonds onto Desdemona's collar sometime that night."

She stood up. "Let's find a phone, gang. I want to call Sean to see who had access to Desdemona during that time."

After returning the newspapers to the librarian, the three girls headed for the phone booth.

Fortunately, Sean had put his phone back on the hook.

"Dunleavy here."

"Hi, it's Nancy Drew. How are you feeling?"

"Better. Have you found my cat?"

"Not yet, but I think I'm closing in. Listen, I have a question for you. Who had access to Desdemona between last Sunday night and the time of your flight on Monday morning?"

Sean was silent for a minute. "Gillian had her that night."

"All night?"

"Pretty much. She wanted to give her a shampoo and manicure—you know, special prep work for the show."

Nancy digested this information eagerly. "Did anyone else have access to Desdemona, besides Gillian?"

"Not that I know of. Why this sudden interest in the events of last Sunday night?"

"Just a hunch," Nancy said vaguely. "Listen, one more thing. I've been wondering about the timing of Desdemona's kidnapping. Why were you all alone in the backstage area just then? Why wasn't it crowded, like it was before the showing of long-haired breeds on Monday?"

"The police asked me the same thing," Sean replied. "It turns out I got the starting time of the showing wrong. I thought it was one o'clock, but it was really two. So, as you can see, I was an hour early, which explains why no one else was there."

"What made you think it was at one?" Nancy asked.

"Let's see, why did I think it was at one? Oh, yes, that's right. Gillian had told me so. She's always making one mistake or another."

Maybe it wasn't a mistake on Gillian's part, Nancy thought. It could have been a deliberate ruse to get Sean alone—so that she could hit him on the head and steal Desdemona!

"Listen, it's very important that I speak to Gillian," Nancy said quickly. "Do you know if she's still at the civic center?"

"I think so," Sean said. "Although actually,

116

she might be gone by now. She was going to take the cats to Le Pet Spa. Then she's heading to Chicago to visit some friends. She'll be back tomorrow morning.''

Nancy frowned. If Gillian was headed for Chicago, she was probably taking the two Persians and the diamonds with her. Maybe she wasn't even going to Chicago, but someplace else altogether—someplace where no one could find her.

Nancy had to stop her before it was too late!

13

Deadly Encounter

"I have to run, Sean," Nancy said. "I'll talk to you later."

After hanging up, Nancy filled Bess and George in on what she had learned from Sean. "I'm going to the civic center now to try to catch Gillian before she leaves town," Nancy said.

"We'll go with you," Bess piped up.

Nancy shook her head. "I'd like you guys to head over to Le Pet Spa. Gillian might be on her way there now, with Sean's cats. And if she *is* there, I need you to stall her however you can. If you can't stall her, then follow her."

"No problem," George said.

After leaving the library, Nancy dropped her friends off at George's house to get a second car, then headed for the civic center as fast as the speed limit would allow.

By the time she got there, dark clouds had started forming in the sky, and a cool wind was blowing, promising rain.

The auditorium was emptying out. It was five minutes to closing time. Making her way against the crowd going in the opposite direction, Nancy rushed to Sean's booth. Gillian was still there.

Nancy immediately slipped behind a nearby booth.

Gillian was going through the motions of packing up for the night. She was putting Sean's cats in portable carriers and straightening up the grooming tools.

The cats were meowing loudly, protesting the carriers.

"Oh, be quiet, you little brats!" Gillian told them in a loud, nasty tone Nancy had never heard her use. Nancy found herself worrying about what kind of care Gillian might be giving Desdemona and Purrfect, wherever they were.

Gillian slipped on a jean jacket, then peered at her watch. "I'll be right back," she told the cats. "Then I'm dropping you off at the kennel for the last time. And do you know what I say to that? Good riddance!"

Gillian hurried off down the aisle. Nancy followed her, marveling at the young woman's change of personality. So she wasn't as shy and sweet as she had appeared, after all.

Gillian headed for a deserted hallway near the refreshment stand. She stopped at a phone booth and dialed a number.

Nancy paused around the corner from where Gillian was standing and studied the situation. Because the hallway was empty, she would have to sneak up on Gillian very slowly and carefully, so as not to be noticed by her.

"Hello, Arnie?" Nancy heard Gillian say. "It's me. I'm sorry I didn't—" Then her voice grew softer, and Nancy couldn't hear any more.

Nancy watched Gillian for a moment. The young woman was intent on her conversation, and her face was half-hidden by her hair. Nancy started down the hall, hugging the wall opposite Gillian's phone booth.

"—don't have the package," Gillian was saying. "Stop yelling and listen to me."

Nancy continued, moving as quietly as she could. Then her hand encountered something— the edge of a doorway. She quickly sneaked into it.

She could now see Gillian clearly and hear every word of her conversation with Arnie, the person on the other end.

"The cat thief managed to get Desdemona today, collar and all," Gillian was saying. "Yes, the collar, too! I tried to get her earlier, but I couldn't, don't you see? I told you before—since the thief stole that other silver Persian on Monday, Sean hasn't let Desdemona out of his sight for two seconds."

There was a pause. "Don't you dare blame me for this," Gillian said after a moment. "I waited to steal Desdemona along with the collar—that was the plan we all agreed on, remember? So we wouldn't get anybody suspicious? It's not my fault that there's some nutty thief on the loose and Sean suddenly decided to play bodyguard with Desdemona."

Listening from her hiding place, Nancy was flushed with excitement. Her diamond-smuggling theory was proving true, and Gillian was as good as confessing to her part in it!

But Nancy's idea that Gillian had stolen the cats herself was going up in smoke. Had a cat thief really thrown a wrench into the smuggler's plans, making off not only with the cats but with the diamond-studded collar?

"All right, fine, we'll figure something out," Gillian was saying, glancing around nervously. "Where do you want to meet? What old warehouse? On Sampson Street? Fine, I'll see you in half an hour."

She hung up abruptly. Nancy instinctively retreated farther into the darkness of the doorway.

She watched as Gillian rushed away, then followed her. Gillian headed back to the booth and picked up the portable carriers. Five minutes later she was out in the parking lot, getting into a silver car.

As Nancy headed for her own car, a crack of lightning flashed brilliantly in the dark sky. A thunderstorm is *not* what I need right now, Nancy said to herself. She jumped into her blue Mustang just as it began to pour, then pulled out of the parking lot after Gillian.

A minute later Gillian raced past Sampson Street without turning into it.

Where is that woman going? Nancy wondered.

Nancy glanced at the clock on the dashboard of her car. Gillian still had twenty minutes until her appointment. She was obviously heading someplace else first—but where? Le Pet Spa was in the other direction. Maybe she was skipping her Sampson Street appointment altogether.

Gillian drove fast. They were near the outskirts of River Heights now, in a neighborhood that was part residential, part industrial. Out of the corner of her eye Nancy saw the blurry images of factories, gas stations, and convenience stores.

A few minutes later Gillian turned into the parking lot of a large brick building. A bright neon sign flashed: THE MERRIWEATHER MOTEL.

The motel was two stories high, with a long balcony on each floor providing entry into the rooms. There was a set of outdoor stairs connecting the first-floor and second-floor balconies. The office was located in a separate, smaller building off to the side.

Nancy parked a little ways from Gillian's car and watched as the young woman climbed the stairs to the second floor, fished a key out of her purse, and went into a door marked 14.

A moment later Nancy got out of her car and went up to the second floor of the motel, to the window of the room Gillian had just entered. The heavy plaid curtains were parted a crack, just enough to provide a view.

She gasped at what she saw. On the bed Gillian was wrestling with two silver Persians, trying to get them into a large cat carrier.

Purrfect and Desdemona!

Nancy's suspicions about Gillian had been right after all. Gillian had lied to Arnie, the person on the phone, about there being a mysterious cat thief on the loose.

Gillian finally got the cats into the cat carrier. Thinking that the young woman would be coming out of her room at any minute, Nancy rushed toward the stairs and down to the first floor. There was a vending machine there. She slipped behind it, and a moment later she heard footsteps clattering down the stairs, accompanied by the sound of meowing.

Nancy peeked from behind the vending machine. Gillian was headed for the motel office building, cat carrier in hand. Just outside the office door she put her load down on the ground and went in.

She was probably checking out, Nancy thought. She was definitely skipping town tonight. But what was she going to do with Purrfect and Desdemona? And where were the diamonds?

A moment later Gillian emerged, picked up the carrier, and headed for her car.

Nancy waited until Gillian had gotten into her car and left the parking lot. Then she rushed to her Mustang and followed.

Driving down the dark, rain-slicked streets, Nancy thought about Gillian's scheme. By telling

Arnie that some cat thief had gotten Desdemona as well as the diamonds, Gillian had clearly double-crossed him. But who was this Arnie? Had Gillian been involved in the London heist? Did she have any partners in her double-cross plan, or was she working alone?

Soon they reached Sampson Street. It was a short, deserted street that dead-ended at the river.

Gillian drove down to the warehouse, which was a seedy-looking building right next to the water. Nancy decided to park around the corner on Packer Street and follow Gillian on foot.

At the corner of Packer and Sampson, Nancy spotted a phone booth. It occurred to her suddenly that she should let someone know where she was. She went into the booth and quickly dialed Bess's number. It was busy. Frustrated, she hung up and tried George. There were several rings, then the answering machine picked up.

"Hi! You have reached the Fayne residence," it began.

Nancy groaned.

"We're sorry we're not here to take your call."

"Oh, please, I'm in a hurry!" Nancy wailed, drumming her fingers impatiently against the glass booth.

"Please leave a message at the sound of the tone, and we'll call you back. Thanks so much." *Beep!*

"George, this is Nancy. This is important.

Gillian has Purrfect and Desdemona with her. I've followed her to the Sampson Street Warehouse, which is at the end of Sampson Street by the river. She's meeting some contact there. I think my theory about the diamonds was right, although I have to make sure."

Nancy saw Gillian go into the warehouse.

"I have to run, George," Nancy said, and hung up.

Nancy left the phone booth and walked briskly to the warehouse. The rain had stopped, but there was a damp chill in the air. Nancy shivered and buttoned her denim jacket.

Sampson Street consisted of a few run-down buildings, a couple of trees, and a single streetlight at the end of the block, in front of the warehouse. The warehouse itself was faded and worn, with yellow paint flaking off. Tall weeds grew around the entrance. A crooked black and white sign read Short and Long-Term Storage.

Somewhere in the distance a dog barked, startling Nancy.

The door to the warehouse was open a crack, and a sliver of light came through. Nancy peeked in. She didn't see Gillian, or her contact, Arnie, although she could hear the dim rumble of voices.

Nancy went in, trying to make as little noise as possible. She found herself in a dark foyer. Just beyond she could see a large room full of boxes. Bare bulbs hung from the ceiling, providing light.

"I'm sorry I'm late, but the roads were bad!" Gillian was saying from somewhere in the large room.

Nancy took off her shoes, set them down on the ground, and tiptoed through the foyer. She could see Gillian now, as well as the person she assumed was Arnie, a big, surly-looking man with red hair and a beard.

Nancy paused at the doorway between the foyer and the large room. She decided to listen to Gillian and Arnie from there, where she would be unnoticed. There were some shelves against the wall holding old paint cans and tools. Nancy hovered beside them.

"Silver is going to be very unhappy about this," Arnie was saying in a deep voice with a hint of a midwestern twang.

Silver, Nancy thought. Where have I heard that name?

"This was your plan, remember?" he continued angrily. "*You* suggested putting the diamonds on that cat's collar. *You* were supposed to keep your eye on the diamonds and the cat until you could steal them both. Silver was counting on you—we were all counting on you. And you go and mess everything up!"

"It was a perfectly good plan!" Gillian retorted. "Think about it, Arnie—smuggling the diamonds out of England on the collar of a cat belonging to a well-known breeder, on its way to America for a big show. The customs officials

126

went through our suitcases, but they hardly gave Desdemona a second glance. It was all going like clockwork until that other cat disappeared. You should have seen Sean after that happened. He wouldn't leave Desdemona alone. There was absolutely no way I could steal her without getting caught."

"You should have figured out something," Arnie grumbled.

"What could I do?" Gillian wailed. "I definitely wasn't going to deviate from our plan and steal just the collar. Like I'd told you all before, that collar was unique, some expensive antique thing. If I'd stolen it, Sean would have missed it right away and reported it to the security people. Then the collar would definitely have been linked to the diamonds, with the timing of our flight out of London and all. By stealing Desdemona, we were going to get her collar without calling attention to it in any way."

Nancy gasped softly. Desdemona's collar *wasn't* unique or expensive. Sean had told her that all his cats had the same kind. Gillian must have lied to her accomplices. But why?

"I figured that the diamonds were safe for a few days on the cat's collar until Sean let down his guard a little and I could get Desdemona. How was I to know the cat thief would beat me to her?" Gillian was saying.

"Excuses, excuses," Arnie said menacingly. "Don't you see? Sob story or no, Silver isn't going to be very understanding about the fact that the diamonds are missing, even if he is your boyfriend.''

Suddenly Nancy remembered. She'd heard the name Silver in the news some time ago. Sam Silver was a renowned English thief and smuggler who had eluded the authorities for years. So Gillian must be his girlfriend!

Nancy was beginning to figure out the details of Gillian's double cross. She must have suggested a plan to her accomplices around the time of the heist. She would replace the rhinestones on Desdemona's collar with the diamonds and smuggle them to America. Then, once at the show, she would steal Desdemona, to make it look as if there were a cat thief loose, and hand over the collar to Arnie. She couldn't steal the collar alone, she'd told them, since it was a "unique" collar and Sean would notice its absence immediately.

But the collar wasn't unique. Gillian had no doubt replaced the diamond-studded collar with a fake collar as soon as she'd arrived in Chicago. She'd then gone ahead with her double cross: stealing Purrfect, then Desdemona, and pretending that it was someone else's doing. And she was acting as if the diamond-studded collar had disappeared along with Desdemona.

All this so Gillian could have the diamonds to herself!

Gillian had really fooled everyone with her timid little assistant bit, Nancy thought. In truth, she was an accomplished actress and a clever schemer—a dangerous combination.

Nancy then wondered where the diamonds were. Did Gillian have them with her or had she hidden them someplace?

"Our only hope is to find the cat thief," Gillian was saying to Arnie.

"I hope whoever it is doesn't realize what's on that collar," Arnie muttered. "For that matter, I hope the diamonds don't fall off."

"Don't worry about that," Gillian replied. "I told you, Louie used to work for a jewelry maker. He mounted those diamonds on there so securely it would take a chisel to pry them off."

"Good," Arnie grumbled.

"I feel responsible for all this," Gillian said. "I've decided to stay in America for a while, to hunt down the thief. I'll give Sean some story or the other—you know, tell him I have to stick around to visit a sick relative."

So that was Gillian's plan, Nancy thought. She was going to buy herself time with her accomplices by staying in America to "hunt down the cat thief." With a few extra days she would have ample opportunity to disappear with the diamonds.

"You don't seem to appreciate the position I'm in," Arnie was saying sulkily. "Silver asked me to line up a customer here. I did, and now he's raring for those diamonds. He gave me half the cash up front—the cash you were going to take back to England. What am I supposed to say to him now? Thanks for your money, but we don't have the diamonds? Some two-bit cat thief has them?"

Just then Nancy accidentally brushed against the shelves she'd been standing next to. A screwdriver came clattering down.

"Hey, what was that?" she heard Arnie cry out.

Nancy glanced around frantically and decided to make a run for the front entrance. But Arnie was too fast for her. He had rushed out to the foyer and spotted Nancy.

"What are you doing here?" Arnie growled, coming toward her.

Nancy froze. Then, thinking quickly, she said, "I have some information for you about the missing Persians."

Gillian had joined Arnie out in the foyer. When she saw Nancy, her mouth dropped open. But she seemed too surprised to say anything.

"Who are you?" Arnie asked Nancy angrily. "What are you doing spying on us?"

When Nancy didn't reply immediately, Arnie picked a rusty crowbar off the shelves and came toward her. His face was dark with menace.

Nancy took a few steps back. But her retreat only fueled Arnie's fury. He lunged forward, grabbed her arm, and pushed her against a wall.

He raised the crowbar in the air. "Tell me who you are, or I'm going to have to get rough!" he warned.

14

Up a Tree

Arnie's grip on her arm tightened. Stay calm, Nancy told herself, staring at the crowbar. Stay calm, and think of a plan to get yourself out of this mess.

Then an idea came to her. Gillian could not afford to have her double cross revealed to Arnie. If Nancy could somehow convey to her that she knew where Desdemona and Purrfect were . . .

"Come on, Gillian, tell him who I am," Nancy called to the young woman. "Tell him that I'm Sam's cousin, Nancy Merriweather, and that I'm helping you find your cat thief."

Hearing the word *Merriweather*—referring to the Merriweather Motel—Gillian started. Good, Nancy thought. She knows I'm onto her.

Gillian smiled nervously at Arnie. "That's

right. She's on the level. She's been helping me out."

Arnie loosened his grip on Nancy's arm slightly. "What do you mean, she's been helping you out? She's not one of us. Does Silver know about this?"

"Well, not exactly, but—" Gillian began.

"I'm his cousin, so I'm sure it'll be okay with him," Nancy interrupted lightly.

"Cousin or not, she's an outsider," Arnie muttered to Gillian. "Why weren't the rest of us informed?"

"I was desperate to find Desdemona and the diamonds!" Gillian insisted. "I called in Nancy just today. She's, um, good at finding people."

Arnie squinted suspiciously at Nancy. "If you're with her, why didn't you tell me right away? Why did you try to escape?"

"I tried to tell you, but before I had a chance you picked up that crowbar," Nancy improvised. "I got scared."

Arnie seemed to consider this for a moment. He let go of her arm. "You'd better be telling the truth."

Nancy rubbed her arm. It felt tender to her touch. She thought about the message she'd left on George's answering machine. If she'd gotten it, she and Bess would be on their way to the warehouse by now. They might have even thought to call the police.

"Why don't we all sit down and come up with a plan together?" Gillian was saying smoothly to

132

Arnie. "We all agree that we have to find the cat thief, right?"

"Sure, sure," Arnie muttered. "I still don't like the idea of this kid being in on—"

At that moment, he happened to notice Nancy's bare feet. "Hey!" he exclaimed. "Why aren't you wearing shoes? Hey, wait a minute!"

Arnie glared at Nancy and Gillian. "You two are trying to pull one over on me here," he growled. "She was sneaking up on me, wasn't she, Gillian? Was she going to come in here and knock me out? Help you escape so you could run off together with the diamonds?"

"No, Arnie," Gillian replied quickly. "You don't understand. We don't have the diamonds—"

"Don't give me that!" Arnie shouted, waving the crowbar in the air. "I want the truth here, and I want it fast! Which one of you is going to talk? Or am I going to have to *make* you talk? I'll start with you, Nancy Merriweather, or whatever your name is. Tell me where the diamonds are, or I'll—"

"Oh, no!" Gillian yelled suddenly, looking over Arnie's shoulder at the front entrance. "The police!"

Arnie whirled around. Gillian took the opportunity to grab a rusty paint bucket from the shelf and swing it at Arnie's head.

"Ugh!" he grunted as he crumpled to the ground.

Gillian turned to Nancy and threw the paint

133

bucket toward her. "Catch!" she cried out with a nasty grin, then ran toward the entrance.

Nancy jumped back to avoid the bucket. It hit the cement floor with a loud bang.

Recovering her composure, Nancy started after Gillian. But just then she noticed something shiny on the floor, a few feet away from Arnie's unconscious body.

She bent down to pick it up. It was a set of keys, held together by a key chain bearing the logo of a car rental agency.

Gillian's car keys, Nancy thought. She must have dropped them while she was reaching for the paint can.

Nancy rushed outside, pausing only to slip on her shoes, which she'd left at the entrance.

Gillian's car was parked next to the river. Gillian was standing next to it, searching frantically through her pockets. The car door was open, and Nancy could hear the meowing of cats from inside. The lone streetlight cast an eerie yellow glow on the scene.

Nancy approached her, keys in hand. "Looking for something?"

Gillian looked up and saw Nancy with the keys.

"How did you—" Gillian began. Then her eyes gleamed, and she reached inside the car. She came out with one of the portable cat carriers.

She walked swiftly over to the river's edge, which was to the side of the warehouse. "Inside this carrier are those precious Persians you've been combing the town for, Purrfect and Desdemona. If you don't throw me my car keys, along with your own, in the next five seconds, these nice cats are going to find themselves at the bottom of the river."

Gillian dangled the carrier over the water and began counting. "One . . . two . . ."

Nancy hesitated, then threw the two sets of car keys at Gillian's feet.

"Good girl," Gillian said, picking up the keys. "Although it's too bad you're so trusting. I was planning to pitch these cats into the river, anyway."

Nancy gasped. "You wouldn't dare."

Gillian lifted the carrier to her face and peeked in. "Goodbye, little darlings," she said. "It's been ever so nice, but—*ouch!*"

One of the cats had reached through the wire mesh door and taken a swipe at Gillian's face. Gillian dropped the carrier, and it fell to the ground. The door swung open, and Purrfect and Desdemona scrambled out. They raced off into the darkness.

At that moment a car came screeching down Sampson Street.

The car stopped behind them, effectively blocking Gillian's escape. Realizing she was outnumbered, Gillian turned and started running down a path along the river.

George leapt out of the car, followed by Bess.

"Nancy, are you all right?" Bess cried. "Where are the police? We called them ages ago."

135

"Well, they're not here yet," Nancy replied. "Listen, you two go after Gillian. Purrfect and Desdemona escaped, and I'm going to try to find them."

George and Bess took off down the path in pursuit of Gillian. Nancy began searching for the two Persians.

"Purrfect! Desdemona! Here, kitties!" Nancy called out loudly. There was a soft meow in response.

"Purrfect! Desdemona!" There was another meow. Nancy realized that it was coming from across the street, although it was too dark to pinpoint the exact location.

She followed the direction of the meow and found herself standing in front of a tall tree. Looking up, she could see the movements of two furry animals among the top branches.

"Purrfect, Desdemona, come on down," Nancy called.

They meowed in response but didn't comply.

"This is just like what happened with Rover." Nancy sighed, remembering her neighbor's kitten that was stuck in the tree. "Unfortunately, I don't happen to have a can of tuna right now."

"Gillian!"

Nancy whirled at the sound of the loud male voice. Arnie was coming out of the warehouse, rubbing his head and glancing around. He had the crowbar in his hand.

"Gillian!" he yelled again. "Gillian, where are

you. You and your sneaky little friend can't hide from me."

Because the only streetlight on the block was in front of the warehouse, Nancy could see Arnie, but he couldn't see her. But she didn't know how long she would remain hidden from his view. He might decide to come across the street at any minute.

But Arnie walked over to the river instead, turning his back toward Nancy. She thought quickly and decided to follow the cats' example and hide in the tree.

She swung nimbly onto a heavy limb. When she'd settled onto it, Purrfect and Desdemona leapt down from their perches and joined her. They rubbed against her, purring.

"Try not to make any noise," Nancy whispered to them, whereupon one of them opened its mouth and let out a loud meow.

Arnie turned from his spot on the riverbank. "What was that?" he growled.

He started coming toward the tree, swinging the crowbar as he marched over. Nancy froze in apprehension.

Arnie was under the tree now, looking up. Both cats meowed at him. He spotted them, then Nancy.

"I've got you now, you diamond thief," he growled. "You'd better come down, or I'll come after you. And when I'm through with you, I'm going after your buddy Gilli—"

The wail of police sirens interrupted him. Two police cars were racing down Sampson Street. They stopped behind Arnie, and four policemen jumped out.

"Freeze!" one of the officers yelled. "Drop that crowbar and raise your hands in the air!"

15

A Happy Reunion

As the officers disarmed Arnie, Nancy climbed down the tree. Purrfect and Desdemona leapt down after her, and she knelt down and petted them. They seemed to know they were safe with her and made no move to scurry away.

"Are you okay, miss?" one of the officers asked her.

"I'm fine," she told him, standing up. Just then she spotted George and Bess coming up the path by the river, holding an angry-looking Gillian between them.

"This is outrageous," Gillian was saying through clenched teeth. When she saw the police, she cried out, "Officers, tell these crazy girls to release me! There's been some mistake."

"It's no mistake," Nancy said, walking up to Gillian and noting her defiant stance. Gillian had certainly changed from the shy, nervous girl Nancy had first met. "Your little scheme has come to an end," Nancy continued. "George, Bess, you can let go of her now. The police will take care of her."

Freed, Gillian stepped toward Nancy and stared at her brazenly. "Maybe you've caught me," she hissed, her eyes flashing. "But you'll never find the diamonds!"

Just then one of the cats jumped up and batted at the pocket of Gillian's jacket. Nancy frowned. She quickly reached into Gillian's pocket.

"Hey!" Gillian cried. "Give that back to me, that's mine!"

Nancy held a cloth ball in the air. "An ordinary cat toy," she announced. "Or should I say, not so ordinary? I don't think catnip stuffing weighs so much."

She ripped open the outer layer of the ball. Several large diamonds fell out. They lay on the ground, sparkling and shimmering brilliantly.

"Now, those are definitely not rhinestones," Nancy said with a smile.

"I don't know how to thank you, Nancy," Andrea said.

After filing a report at the police station, Nancy and her friends had driven to Andrea's house with Purrfect and Desdemona. The girls were sitting in her living room with mugs of hot coffee. The two cats were chasing each other around the house, meowing loudly.

"They've gotten to be pretty chummy, haven't they?" George remarked. "Maybe Desdemona won't want to go back to Sean. Maybe she'd rather stay here with you and Purrfect."

"Wouldn't Sean love that," Andrea said, chuckling. "Does he know what's happened, by the way?"

"I called him from the police station," Nancy replied. "He would have come down, but he's still recuperating. I promised him that I'd deliver Desdemona to him at his hotel after seeing you." She paused, then added, "He was incredibly shocked about Gillian."

"I think that if it weren't for his gigantic ego, he would have suspected her long ago," George said dryly. "He just couldn't see that his submissive little assistant was plotting behind his back."

"It *is* hard to believe that Gillian is our cat thief," Andrea murmured. "She seemed so nice."

"I know it," Nancy replied, cradling the warm mug in her hands. "It was an incredibly clever scheme—stealing Purrfect first, to set up the idea that there was a cat-napper on the loose. Gillian figured her accomplices would never suspect her when Desdemona and the diamonds vanished."

"So did she just pick up Purrfect and walk out of the civic center with her?" Andrea asked.

"As simple as that," Nancy replied. "While you were off getting your grooming tools, Gillian walked into the backstage area, picked up

Purrfect's carrier, then went out the blue door into the parking lot. She kept her there in the back seat of her car, hidden under some shopping bags, until she could get her to the Merriweather Motel—during one of her famous long breaks, of course."

"Gillian must have caught onto you right away, Nan," George remarked. "Minutes after you started snooping around the civic center, she sneaked that note into your pocket."

"And she really managed to get us sidetracked with all that stuff about Sean," Bess piped up. "She got *me* sidetracked, anyway. That is, until I, um, started pursuing the Kara Kramer angle."

George grinned mischievously. "How *is* that Kara Kramer angle, by the way? Have you got another date with Neal any time soon?"

Bess turned bright red. Everybody laughed.

"Seriously, though, Gillian had me believing her Sean story, too," Nancy said. "Looking back, I can see why she had to set him up. After Purrfect's disappearance, Sean got so paranoid about Desdemona. He was hovering over her constantly. Gillian hadn't counted on that, and it threw a big wrench into her plans. She had to buy herself time—"

"—to get her hands on Desdemona. Therefore, the setup," George finished.

"But didn't you say you saw Sean, or someone who looked like Sean, watching you from the terrace right before that pot of geraniums fell on your head?" Andrea asked. "That seemed genuinely fishy. Plus, what about those matches you found?"

"Gillian confessed to all that at the police station," Nancy began.

"*Confessed* isn't exactly the word," Bess interrupted. "Wheeled and dealed is more like it. That Gillian is so wily. She had the police and the district attorney sending faxes to London within minutes. She said that she'd tell all about her British smuggling buddies, and about her own double-cross scheme, if the British government promised to go easy on her."

Andrea shook her head and said, "Wow." Then she turned to Nancy. "You were saying about the matches?"

Nancy nodded. "If you'll recall, she'd sent me a note telling me to meet her on the terrace at nine o'clock. Well, she'd gone out there ten minutes earlier, and I guess Sean had followed her—out of curiosity, or to ask her a question, or something. She wasn't sure. By the time he got out there, she was already hiding up on the second-floor balcony."

"Getting ready to knock you senseless with a flowerpot," Bess said, shuddering.

Nancy took a sip of coffee. "She had it all arranged. She'd placed the River Inn matchbook right under the balcony, knowing I was bound to notice it and pick it up. And when I did, she pushed the pot off the ledge."

"And then Tad found you," Andrea said.

"Right," Nancy said. "Anyway, you can probably guess the rest. Gillian raced from the balcony into the second-floor hallway, down a set of stairs, and back into the ballroom. A few minutes after nine she came rushing through the French doors.''

"Acting all worried and surprised," George remarked sarcastically.

"And claiming that she'd seen Sean hovering just *inside* the French doors at exactly nine, to make him seem even more guilty," Nancy added. "When I asked her later about the matchbook, she managed to pass that off on him, too, although not in any obvious or pushy way. She told me very vaguely that she thought he smoked a pipe."

"Did you ever find out why she stole Desdemona the way she did?" Andrea asked. "I mean, why knock Sean out?"

"Nancy had that figured out ages ago," Bess said proudly. "Well, hours ago, anyway."

"Gillian told us all about it," Nancy said. "With Sean not letting Desdemona out of his sight, and Arnie and her other accomplices putting the pressure on her, Gillian had to act fast. So she came up with a plan to get Sean and Desdemona alone. She told him the wrong time for the Persian showing, and he showed up early. There wasn't anybody else around. Then, Gillian sneaked up behind him and conked him on the head with a folding chair."

"Ugh," Andrea said, grimacing.

"Gillian then wrapped Desdemona in a raincoat and went dashing out the blue door. She didn't have time to put her in a carrier. But Desdemona struggled a lot." Nancy paused and called to Desdemona, who was wrestling with Purrfect on the carpet. Desdemona looked up with her big blue eyes. Thinking food was being offered, she shook herself free of the other cat and came over to Nancy. Purrfect, not wanting to be left out, followed.

Nancy pointed to Desdemona's collar. "See? One of the rhinestones is missing. While she was squirming in Gillian's arms, the rhinestone got knocked loose and fell to the ground."

Desdemona and Purrfect, realizing that nothing edible was being made available, meowed in protest and returned to their wrestling match.

"It's lucky it did, too," Nancy continued. "If I hadn't found it, I might never have solved this mystery. It helped me to make the connection between the cats' disappearance and the London heist."

"I guess this means the dark-haired woman running out the back exit *was* Gillian," George said.

"Right," Nancy replied. "Once she put Desdemona in her car, she came running back into the civic center with a bottle of grooming powder in her hand. She put on quite an act when she saw Sean lying on the ground."

"That woman should win an Academy Award," George commented wryly. "She's a great actress!"

"Then, right after that, she went back out to her car, took Desdemona to the Merriweather Motel, and came back," Nancy said. "The security guards actually stopped her on the way out of the parking lot, but she told them she was Sean's assistant, and that she was rushing over to the hospital to be with him. They let her go right away, without even noticing the bundle in her backseat."

"Amazing," Andrea murmured.

"Hours later I went back to the civic center and started following her around," Nancy continued. "And you all know the rest."

"And now it's way past dinnertime. Why don't we go to Pepe's Pizza and celebrate?" Bess suggested brightly.

"First, we have to get Desdemona back to Sean." Nancy smiled. "That is, if we can pry her and Purrfect apart."

Exhausted from their wrestling, the two cats were curled up together, fast asleep.

"I'm glad there's no more mystery to solve," Bess said cheerfully. "Now we can act like normal, boring spectators."

It was the final day of the cat show, and Nancy, George, and Bess were heading for gallery six, where the Grand Competition was to be held shortly.

"Since when do 'normal, boring spectators' wear their favorite red dress to a cat show?" George teased.

Bess glanced down. "This old thing?" she said casually. "It's just something I happened to throw on this morning."

"Uh-huh," George replied. "Is Neal going to be at the Grand Competition, by any chance?"

Bess shot her a look. "How would I know? I mean, he probably is, since Purrfect is Simon-Ross Media's star cat and all that."

"Ms. Drew!"

Kara Kramer was rushing up to them, waving a handbag in the air. "Ms. Drew, I've been looking all over the place for you!"

"How are you, Ms. Kramer?" Nancy said politely. "You remember my friends Bess and George."

Kara barely acknowledged them. "Ms. Drew, I have a proposition for you. I want to put you in the next Kitty Classics commercial—you and Purrfect. What do you think?"

"Me, in a commercial?" Nancy repeated. "Thank you, but I don't think—"

"But you don't understand," Kara interrupted excitedly. "The publicity, dear girl, the publicity! We have to capitalize on your sensational capture of the jewel thieves and your heroic rescue of poor Purrfect in the face of grave danger. People will flock to the stores to buy Kitty Classics when they see you on television."

Bess elbowed Nancy. "Detective turned TV star. Sounds pretty cool, Nan."

"I appreciate your thinking of me, Ms. Kramer, but I really don't think so," Nancy said. "I need to keep a low profile as a detective. I can't have people all over America knowing what I look like."

But Kara was not taking no for an answer. "Promise me that you'll consider it," she said, pressing a business card into Nancy's hand. "I must be off. See you at the Grand Competition!"

She turned and rushed down the aisle, waving her handbag at somebody else.

Nancy glanced at her watch. "Hey, we'd better get moving ourselves. The competition is starting in just a few minutes."

The three girls made their way to gallery six and found seats next to Winona Bell. Neal was sitting up front with his coworkers. When he spotted Bess, he waved enthusiastically, and she waved back.

"You!" Winona exclaimed, squinting at Nancy. "I heard about what you did, tracking down those Persians. Is that what you do for a living, find missing cats?"

"Not exactly," Nancy replied, chuckling.

"What about those jewel thieves?" Winona persisted. "What happened to them?"

"Well, Gillian Samms, the one who stole the cats, cooperated with the police and gave them a lot of information about her accomplices," Nancy explained. "With her help, the English police were able to round up the head of the gang, Sam Silver, and all the rest of them. Gillian has been extradited to England, where she'll stand trial.

And the gang's American contact, Arnie, will stand trial in Chicago."

"It's just like the movies, isn't it?" Winona marveled. "Cops and robbers!"

"How are you feeling, Ms. Bell?" Bess piped in.

"Oh, much better, thank you, young lady. Especially since I got myself a Persian of my own."

She reached under her seat and dragged out a portable carrier. Inside was a small caramel-colored kitten playing with its tail.

"How sweet!" Bess cried. "Where did you get him? Or her?"

"It's a her," Winona replied. "Her mother is one of the cats at this show. This one's going to be a winner in a year or two, I can tell."

Just then a man came out on the stage and tapped on the microphone. "Ladies and gentlemen, the Grand Competition is about to start. Please take your seats."

Two dozen cat owners filed out of the backstage area with their just-groomed cats. Andrea was among them, as was Sean.

Andrea spotted Nancy and her friends and smiled nervously at them. They smiled back encouragingly.

After the judge examined the cats, he took an unusually long time to reach his decision. Finally, he held up a blue ribbon and pinned it on Purrfect's cage.

The audience broke into applause. Bess and Nancy cheered loudly, and George whistled.

The judge then pinned the red ribbon, for second place, on Desdemona's cage. Third place went to a young Burmese cat.

The three girls rushed up to the stage to congratulate Andrea. When they got there, Sean was shaking Andrea's hand.

"Congratulations," he was saying to her. Nancy saw that he was even smiling.

Tad joined them just then. "I just got here," he said breathlessly. "I got held up at the store. Nice going, honey." He put his arm around Andrea, and she looked up at him, beaming.

Nancy, Bess, and George glanced at each other. Andrea noticed and said, "This whole ordeal over Purrfect has, um, brought Tad and me closer together. We've decided that the three of us should be a family again."

"That's great!" Nancy said happily, and George and Bess added their congratulations.

Purrfect and Desdemona, still in their cages, began meowing angrily.

"I think they're feeling left out," Andrea remarked, extracting Purrfect. Sean took Desdemona out of her cage. The two cats spotted each other and wriggled impatiently, wanting to play.

"These cats are going to have to become pen pals or something," George joked. "They really like each other."

Andrea turned to Nancy. "None of this would

150

have been possible if it hadn't been for you. How can I thank you for finding Purrfect?"

"And Desdemona," Sean added.

"It wasn't all my doing," Nancy said modestly. "I had a few terrific helpers."

"In honor of you girls, I'm going to name Purrfect's future kittens Nancy, Bess, and George," Andrea declared.

Everybody broke into laughter.

"That's the nicest compliment I've ever had," Nancy said, and Bess and George nodded in agreement.

NANCY DREW® MYSTERY STORIES By Carolyn Keene